'I'm rather deeply i

Lucy gave Robert w
appealing look. He w
policy proved vain.

He returned her look quizzically. 'Yes, you are, aren't you?' he agreed.

There was a stunned silence while Lucy tried to think of a dignified retort. At last she abandoned the attempt. 'There's no need to sound so *pleased* about it,' she said crossly.

Dear Reader

Wouldn't it be wonderful to drop everything and jet off to Australia—the land of surf, sunshine, 'barbies' and, of course, the vast, untamed Outback? Mills & Boon contemporary romances offer you that very chance! Tender and exciting love stories by favourite Australian authors bring vividly to life the city, beach and bush, and introduce you to the most gorgeous heroes that Down Under has to offer. . .check out your local shops, or with our Readers' Service, for a trip of a lifetime!

The Editor

Born in London, **Sophie Weston** is a traveller by nature who started writing when she was five. She wrote her first romance recovering from illness, thinking her travelling was over. She was wrong, but she enjoyed it so much that she has carried on. These days she lives in the heart of the city with two demanding cats and a cherry tree—and travels the world looking for settings for her stories.

Recent titles by the same author:

GYPSY IN THE NIGHT
WIFE TO CHARLES

GOBLIN COURT

BY
SOPHIE WESTON

MILLS & BOON LIMITED
ETON HOUSE 18–24 PARADISE ROAD
RICHMOND SURREY TW9 1SR

First published in Great Britain 1976
by Mills & Boon Limited

© Sophie Weston 1976

Australian copyright 1992
Philippine copyright 1992
This edition 1992

ISBN 0 263 77580 1

Set in Plantin 10 on 12 pt.
01-9206-48416

Typeset in Great Britain by County Typesetters, Kent

Made and printed in Great Britain

CHAPTER ONE

LUCY ran down the lane to the village school. There was no pavement and the road was slippery with a coating of wet fallen leaves. Once or twice she skidded dangerously. She flung a harassed glance at her watch. Four o'clock already, and the children came out of their last class at a quarter to four. They would be worried as they always were when she was late. And Miss Frobisher would be impatient to lock up the school.

She had a stitch in her side and she slowed, breathing hard. Really, it was ridiculous to be afraid of the children's teacher. But she could not deny that she was. The prospect of Miss Frobisher's displeasure spurred her to further efforts and she began to trot again.

Suddenly and unexpectedly she heard the sound of a powerful car engine behind her. She had only time to recall amazedly that nothing came down the lane but the farm lorry or, occasionally, Colonel Browning's Land Rover before it swept round the curve. She leapt ungracefully for the ditch. The grass was damp and she had to cling to a vigorous growth of stinging nettles to prevent herself sliding down into what, augmented by the autumn rains, was now a swift-flowing brook.

'Damn!' she said, pardonably.

The car had swung itself to a halt and the driver got out. He looked round, saw her and strolled across. Insulted by his lack of urgency, Lucy glared at him.

From her undignified position he looked immensely tall. He was wearing dark glasses, ludicrously unnecessary in the early evening murk, she thought. Behind them he appeared to be frowning. In ordinary circumstances a confrontation with an irate stranger would have sent Lucy into a panic. But now she was wet, cold and late and had had a severe fright on top of it. To crown it all the detestable man stood over her without offering to help her to her feet. He even looked as if he was laughing. It occurred to her that she must look ridiculous, like some collapsed puppet sprawled at the side of the road. She struggled up furiously.

His lips twitched. 'I take it you're all right? I don't see any blood or dismembered limbs.'

'Small thanks to you,' she snapped. She held out an imperative hand. 'Well, help me up, then.'

Ignoring the flapping hand, he bent, sliding his arms round her, and brought her very competently to her feet. He stood her up on the road, retaining a hold on her arm as if he thought she would topple over if he let her go, and began to dust her down solicitously.

Lucy gritted her teeth. 'Thank you,' she said with restraint when he had finished.

'Not at all. You were very muddy. Do you,' he inquired interestedly, 'like mud?'

'I prefer it to being flattened by fast cars,' she retorted. Glancing at the car, she saw it was of the low, sporting variety favoured by her brother. It was also, she noted with some satisfaction, liberally coated with mud.

He raised his eyebrows. 'Flattened? Do you mean you thought I'd run you over? Was *that* the reason for your dramatic nose-dive? I see. I am,' he added, by far too late, 'sorry.'

'You are too kind,' said Lucy with awful politeness.

He chuckled. 'Oh, dear! I truly am sorry. But there was no need for you to leap out of my way so dramatically, you know. The car stops on a sixpence and I wasn't going fast.'

Lucy sniffed. 'Speed is relative. Most of the traffic on this road is four-footed.'

He sighed. 'All right, I was going fast by local standards. I would still have missed you by a mile.'

'It didn't feel like that. I had the impression that you were definitely breathing down my neck.'

'I'm sorry,' he said again without any recognisable signs of penitence. He held her away from him and looked at her as if he had never seen such a thing before and found it interesting.

'You don't sound sorry,' said Lucy militantly, taking exception to the appraising look.

'I mean,' he explained carefully, 'that I'm sorry you're so—er—jumpy.'

'Oh!' It was a squeak of rage. She whisked out of his hands. 'How dare you?'

He was shaking with laughter. 'I hardly know,' he admitted. 'Allow me to give you a lift to wherever you're going and we'll discuss it.'

'I will not,' said Lucy smartly.

He shook his head reprovingly. 'You're not very civil.'

'No,' she agreed complacently. 'I'm late.' She looked at her watch and found that the dial was covered with green stains. Underneath it seemed to indicate ten past four. The children would be frantic. 'Excuse me, I must go. I have to pick the children up from school.'

She turned away and her forgotten stitch stabbed. Lucy winced. At once he took her elbow, frowning.

'You *are* hurt.'

'It's nothing. It's not even,' she admitted grudgingly, 'your fault. I was running and I had a stitch.'

He laughed. 'Well, that's honest. Still, I can't let you trudge on up this extremely muddy lane. Especially as I seem to have stampeded you into the ditch in the first place. Get into the car and I'll drive you to this school of yours.'

'It's not far,' she objected.

He strode over to the car and opened the passenger door. 'Get in.'

Lucy shrugged. 'Oh, very well,' she said with bad grace. 'It's straight ahead on the left. About half a mile further on.'

He settled himself in his own seat and strapped the safety belt across his body. Lucy, who had a running battle with the children to make them use the seat belts, was impressed.

'Thank you,' he said solemnly, and drove on.

The children were waiting for her. There was no sign of Miss Frobisher. For a moment Lucy wondered indignantly if she could have locked up and gone home leaving them on their own, but dismissed it instantly. They had obviously been forbidden to go out on to the road, with the result that they were standing on the low wall round the playground. This meant that they were, at least in their own eyes, technically still within the school ground while still able to watch the road. Lucy knew enough of their psychology by now to feel sure that they would not have bothered to observe even so much of the prohibition if the threatening Miss Frobisher had not been lurking somewhere in the background.

Boy, his too-small cap set rakishly on his curly head, was perambulating the wall with his arms flung wide to balance him and an expression of intense concentration. Lucy, knowing the wall was quite three feet wide, felt no anxiety.

Angela, on the other hand, was standing still with her own and Boy's satchels at her feet, staring down the road with painful intensity. Her round little face looked pinched—with more than the bitter wind, Lucy thought compassionately. It was Angela's abiding terror that her aunt would desert her.

'Here,' she said to the man, her eyes on Angela.

'Is that one yours? The little one looking like a terrier on a leash?'

'Yes, she's one of mine,' Lucy replied absently.

Angela, at first uninterested in the car, had now noticed that it was slowing down and her eyes widened. As they drew up and Lucy hopped out she began to struggle off the wall. The satchels fell squashily into the weedy verge. Angela ignored them.

'Daddy!' she cried, pelting across to the car.

Lucy froze. Why on earth hadn't she thought what the sight of that car would suggest to the children? Hadn't she herself thought it looked like Peter's? Horrified, she watched the little tableau.

Her rescuer, in the process of getting out of the car when Angela cried out, nimbly swung round, slamming the door behind him, and caught her in her headlong rush. He swung her high in the air, laughing.

'I'm afraid not,' he said nicely, 'but lucky Daddy.' He put her down gently. 'Is it only daddies who get the twenty-one-gun salute?' He looked at Lucy. 'Don't mothers qualify?'

Angela was disappointed and, as always when she was upset, began to pout. 'That's not my mother,' she said disparagingly. 'That's only Lucy.'

'Oh,' he said rather blankly.

Lucy felt sorry for him. 'Angela is my niece,' she explained. 'She and her brother are living with me at the moment. That's her brother,' nodding to the absorbed Boy, 'doing the high wire act over there.'

'I see.' He looked from Boy to Angela. 'Well, they seem reasonably sized. We should be able to stow them and their satchels in the back and I'll take you home. I assume that is where you're bound?'

Lucy struggled with her pride. It would be heaven not to have to walk the mile and a half home with the reproachful children trailing behind. Nevertheless, pride would have won if Miss Frobisher had not chosen that moment to make her appearance.

The village school had only two classes which housed thirty or so children. The juniors were taught by a motherly lady who was as old as the school itself. The seniors, among whom were Boy and Angela, were in Miss Frobisher's class. She was an athletic young woman with exquisitely cut blonde hair and diamanté-rimmed spectacles. She terrorised her charges, even tough little Billy Marshall from the farm. Angela and Lucy were petrified of her. Boy regarded her as something of a nuisance. But even Boy did not disobey her.

'Ah, Miss Wild,' said the dragon, locking the outer

door of the school with much jingling of keys. 'Were you held up?' Without raising her voice she added menacingly, 'We *don't* walk on walls, Gerard.'

Philosophically Boy abandoned his pastime and came over to Lucy, who was apologising in a flustered way.

'I was late leaving Colonel Browning and then I—er—fell over in the lane. This gentleman scraped me up and brought me the rest of the way.'

Her audience reacted variously. Her rescuer did his best to look modest while Miss Frobisher turned her glasses on him interestedly. The martial light went out of her eyes. She smiled at him, looking, to Lucy's surprise, quite human, and ignored the others as she asked him whether he had lost his way in the village.

Angela slipped a cold hand into Lucy's. Boy surveyed her.

'Were you hurt?' he asked.

'I don't think so.' Rather vaguely Lucy looked down at her muddy coat. To her surprise she found that the hem looked as if it were stained with blood. Pulling it aside, she found a sizeable graze and some impressive bruising on her right knee. Boy was impressed. He was a connoisseur of bruises, but this was one of the finest specimens he had seen in a long time. His own knees were permanently chipped. Gravely he compared Lucy's hurts with his own latest crop and regretfully decided that Lucy's were superior.

'Miss Wild,' said Jane Frobisher coldly.

Lucy jumped. 'Oh! Er—yes, Miss Frobisher?'

'I'm sorry you were hurt. And of course, in the circumstances, it couldn't be helped. But you did say you were already late. That's the third time this week, Miss

Wild. I really can't have the children hanging round the school till all hours. You really must try to leave on time.'

Lucy hung her head guiltily. 'Yes, Miss Frobisher.'

'After all, I can't guarantee to be free to stay with them every evening.'

'No, Miss Frobisher.'

The man took a hand. 'Quite true. And we're taking up too much of your time now we have arrived,' he said proprietorially. He ignored Lucy's indignant stare. 'If the children will fetch their bags we'll be off and not keep you any longer.'

Miss Frobisher looked chagrined. Clearly this was not quite what she had meant. Lucy, looking bewilderedly from one to the other, saw that Miss Frobisher was more than prepared to continue her conversation with the stranger, no matter how time-consuming it might prove. He, however, was blandly stuffing the children inside the car and bidding her a charming goodbye. Perforce, Lucy followed.

The children were enchanted to be driven away from school. Lucy, who husbanded petrol like a miser, seldom collected them in her own ancient runabout. Boy, squirming round so he could look out of the rear window, raised his hand in a gracious farewell to the receding Miss Frobisher.

'Whew!' observed their driver, when she was out of sight. 'I'll bet she's a great disciplinarian.' He looked sideways down at Lucy. 'Did she teach you too?'

'*Jane Frobisher*?' Lucy was honestly amazed. 'Good heavens, no. She's younger than I am.'

That sideways, enigmatic look again. 'No one would guess it,' he murmured.

'Oh?' Lucy, who had been calming down, began to bristle again. She suspected an insult. 'Why?'

'Oh, this and that. Just an impression. Tell me, where am I taking you?'

'Where are you going?' she countered.

'Ultimately Windrush Manor, if I can find it.'

'Oh!' She was startled. The house in question had been empty for over a year ever since the previous owner had died. The village had been filled with rumours that the heirs had tried to persuade the National Trust to buy it. It was a fine Jacobean house, small but, until recently, beautifully preserved. However, after the death of old Mrs Appleton it had fallen into neglect through disuse. The village had shaken its head over the grounds, which had rapidly gone to seed. There was speculation on the state of the house itself. It was generally agreed that Mrs Appleton had let it go in her last years, poor soul, and that it would cost vast sums to restore it to a habitable state. And if it were not done soon then there would be nothing for it but to pull the old house down which— again opinion was united—would be a tragedy.

'Do you know it?'

Lucy, who had spent much of her childhood playing in Mrs Appleton's elaborate garden, smiled sadly. 'Yes, I know it. It's by the river. I suppose it's quite difficult to find. There's a gate into the knot garden that opens out of the churchyard—that's the way I always used to go in. But there's a drive which goes down to the house through the home wood. You should have carried on through the village for a couple of miles.'

He seemed taken aback. 'So far? But I thought the house was in the village.'

'So it is – the house itself. But the villagers all get to it through the churchyard, or along the river path. You can't take a car either way.'

'But two *miles*. The home wood, you say. Does all that land go with the house?'

'It used to. I think Colonel Browning bought it from Mrs Appleton years ago. But there's still a right of way through it to the house, though I don't know what state the drive will be in by now.'

'It can't be worse than your local roads,' he observed. 'I shall risk it.'

'They were cutting some trees down in the home wood last weekend,' volunteered Angela from the back. 'Rusty and I went down there for conkers and Mr Barton told us we couldn't stay because they were going to fell that big one by the gate.'

'That wasn't to clear the drive, stupid,' said Boy from the superiority of eight years old. 'That was because the tree was ill and they didn't want it to spread. That's right, isn't it, Lucy?'

Because Lucy did a certain amount of secretarial work for Colonel Browning the children automatically assumed that she knew as much about his land as he did himself. In fact, although she had been born and brought up in the country, it was the children, new to it a year ago, who knew more about the land and its seasons, the local places and of course the local people. Lucy sometimes felt that she was living with the two most arrant gossips in a village not short of them.

'I don't know,' she said now. 'And you know I don't like you taking Rusty out on your own.'

Rusty was an amiable but overgrown Irish wolfhound

who belonged to Nicholas Browning at the Royal Oak. Angela, although she loved all animals, was a little afraid of Rusty and only took him for walks as part of a well-laid campaign to induce Lucy to admit a dog to Hazel Cottage.

Angela began to pout and, glancing in his driving mirror, the man intervened.

'What's wrong with the trees? Dutch elm disease?'

Lucy sighed. 'I suppose so. There was an outbreak in the copse on the hill, but I know Colonel Browning was hoping it wouldn't get down to the valley.'

'Who is this Colonel Browning? The local squire?'

She chuckled. 'You could put it like that.'

'Lucy works for him,' announced Angela importantly.

He came to the end of the road and stopped altogether. 'Now where?' he said helplessly.

'Turn right, then go straight through the village. If you would drop us at the shop, I would be very grateful. Then you go out past the bus stop and the Royal Oak.'

'Thank you. And is this driveway signposted?'

'I'm not sure.' Lucy turned in her seat. 'Do you remember, Angela?'

'Not for sure.'

'I'm afraid we're not very helpful natives,' she said ruefully. 'I never really notice the things round me. All I do remember is that it's very dark and sort of overhung with laurel or rhododendron or something. Oh, and there's a pair of old iron gates.'

'Shut?'

'Of course not,' she said, shocked. 'They haven't been shut as long as I can remember.'

'Then they will undoubtedly be covered with creeper and totally unrecognisable as ironware. It sounds dismal—like the Sleeping Beauty's Castle,' he added for Angela's benefit. Angela continued to regard him warily. 'And is the entrance on the right or the left?'

'Oh, the left, down towards the river. The house is pretty well on the bank, you know. That's why it's called Windrush Manor.'

'I'm glad to hear it,' he said austerely.

'Why?' demanded Angela.

'Because otherwise it sounds like something out of a Gothic fairytale.'

Angela didn't know what Gothic meant, but she knew about fairytales and approved of them. Her suspicion abated, she retired again to her cramped corner of the car.

'Oh, there's the shop,' said Lucy in relief. 'If you'd just stop here. . .'

But he was pulling across the road to stop outside it.

'There's no need. . .' she began, but he interrupted her.

'There's every need if I'm going to eat tonight, to say nothing of tomorrow morning. Or will they refuse to serve me because I ran you down?'

'Don't talk nonsense,' she snapped, embarrassed. 'It simply didn't occur to me you would want to do any shopping.'

He looked amused. 'Why on earth not? Did you think I was going to live on owl's eggs and baboon's blood just because I'm staying at Goblin Court?'

'I didn't think about it at all,' she said loftily, slightly spoiling her effect by adding, 'You didn't say you were going to *stay* there.'

'Well, I am. And, though I don't want to hurry you, it

looks to me as if the shop is in immediate danger of closing. Ought we not to stake a claim before they pull down the blinds?'

'Oh, yes, of course.' Lucy discovered she was staring at him in a very rude way and tore her eyes away, blushing. She bundled out of the car and ran into the shop, knowing that Mr and Mrs Lamb would take due note of her arrival in an unknown car with a stranger and that neither those facts nor her flushed cheeks and bright eyes would lose anything in the telling.

She plunged immediately into buying muffins and black cherry jam with a businesslike desperation.

The children and the stranger followed her into the shop. He looked round casually while she made her purchases and Boy, who seemed to feel that they were slightly responsible for the man's well-being, explained to him that he would need a substantial supply of peanuts, chocolate digestive biscuits and pineapple juice to enable him to bear the rigours of Windrush Manor. Mrs Lamb, serving Lucy with butter and cheese in a perfunctory way, kept a smiling eye and both ears trained on the more interesting conversation.

At last, exasperated, Lucy said, 'Perhaps you would like to serve this gentleman first.'

It was accepted with alacrity. 'Well, of course, you're in no hurry, Lucy m'dear.' And she was ignored thereafter.

Although he didn't take all of Boy's freely offered advice, he did buy a gratifying amount, including a supply of potato crisps that made the children's eyes widen with awe and admiration. He also bought an enormous tin of instant coffee which Mrs Lamb usually stocked for Mrs Browning, who held coffee mornings.

'Do you think you'll be staying long hereabouts?' she asked, as she packed his purchases into a large cardboard box.

He looked at the large tin in his hand and smiled. 'I just drink a lot of coffee,' he said gently.

Lucy hid a smile. Although she was still seething from their original encounter she could not deny that his handling of Mrs Lamb was masterly. He parried her every question, but so politely that she did not seem to realise that she was not actually acquiring any information. After ten minutes of interchange she had still not even elicited his name. Lucy, who had all her life been a victim of the Lambs' kindly prying, admired his technique. While Mrs Lamb added up his bill painstakingly, she surveyed him dispassionately for the first time.

Her first impression of height was confirmed. He towered above the children in the crowded little shop, oddly out of place, and she realised suddenly that he was dressed for a warmer climate. Besides his dark glasses he was dressed in jeans and a light cotton shirt open at the throat as if for coolness. Not much of his face was visible and the glasses masked all expression. He was leaning negligently against Mrs Lamb's marble-topped counter, ignoring the children who were skipping round him. When presented with the bill he pulled a cheque book out of his back pocket. With it came a little book that fell with a plop on the spotless floor. Angela retrieved it.

'That's a passport,' she told him kindly. 'You mustn't lose it or you can't go home. My daddy's got one and so have Boy and I.'

'Thank you,' he said briefly, stuffing it unceremoniously back into his pocket.

Such unconcern worried Angela. 'You mustn't lose it,' she repeated urgently.

'I won't.'

Mrs Lamb, bright-eyed, waited hopefully, but Angela subsided. The man did not seem disposed to offer any explanation of why he travelled around England with his passport in his pocket. Her eyes met Lucy's in excited speculation. Ashamed, Lucy looked away. She was as bad as the rest of the village, she thought disgustedly. As if she didn't know how painful even the most kindly meant inquisitiveness could be.

Her gaze came back to him. He had an oddly remote face: high cheekbones, dark glasses and an intemperate mouth. It was a formidable aspect. The dark glasses, she found, were regarding her steadily. Illogically, it seemed to her that such blatant staring was rude. Deliberately she put up her brows, returning his survey. One corner of that mouth quivered and was ruthlessly controlled.

'Well, I seem to have everything for the moment,' he said cheerfully. 'Thank you for setting me on my way. Goodbye.'

The children watched him stow his box of groceries in the car with some wistfulness. His idea of essential foodstuffs seemed to them more realistic than their aunt's.

Mrs Lamb shared their regret at his departure. 'Still,' she said philosophically, 'I suppose we'll be seeing more of him. If he's to move into the Manor, that is.'

The last was clearly a question. Lucy said sharply that she had no idea what his plans were or—forestalling further questioning—who he was.

'Come along,' she said to the children. 'Mrs Lamb wants to shut up shop and it's time we had tea, or you'll never get round to your homework.'

They groaned, but they followed her goodhumouredly enough. Mrs Lamb saw them out of the shop with a cheery smile. They heard the bolt pushed to behind them and the blinds were down and the lights switched off before they were out of sight.

The grey evening was darkening, not unpleasantly. Angela took Lucy's hand while Boy dashed ahead, his satchel bumping about on his back like a muleteer's pack. He seemed not to notice it. Lucy looked down at Angela.

'Are you tired?' she said.

The little girl shook her head and skipped a couple of steps as if to prove it. 'Can we go and see Uncle Nicholas?' she hazarded hopefully.

'You mean, can we go and see Rusty,' said Lucy. She sighed resignedly. 'Oh, very well, I suppose so, but not for long. Uncle Nicholas will be busy and you both have homework to do this evening.'

Angela ignored this puritanical rider and danced off to join Boy. They both then began to run towards the Royal Oak. This old inn stood at the end of the village where it looked rather like a gingerbread cottage. Its looks belied it. In fact it belonged to Nicholas Browning, the energetic nephew of Lucy's employer. He had bought it some five years previously when it was a simple village pub and in that time had succeeded in turning it into one of the best restaurants in the county. A succession of temperamental chefs and delectable waitresses had augmented the small rural community in those years so that the enterprise was generally thought to be a good thing except by those diehards who did not like to see their habitual home from home invaded by, as they put it, town types. But as Nicholas was particularly careful to maintain both the fire and the service in the snug where these worthies congregated at particularly generous levels, hostilities seldom broke out.

On the whole the village contented itself with remarking, whenever the subject arose, that he must have spent a mint 'o money on the old place. Which indeed, as Lucy, who did a certain amount of work for him, well knew, he had. Rather too much in her judgement. Nicholas Browning had a sanguine temperament and a good deal of charm with he exercised to very good effect on his creditors. However, on several occasions he had had to borrow money from his uncle in order to weather a passing crisis. Lucy could imagine that, now that the summer trade had fallen off and the Christmas trade not yet begun, another crisis was in the offing. And this time, she also knew, Colonel Browning would be very hard put to it to help. She had tried to hint something of the sort to Nicholas, for she was very fond of his uncle and rather more than fond of the amiable young man himself, but without any notable success.

A faint frown creased her brows. The children were tumbling into the back yard of the Royal Oak and she followed at a more sedate pace. Of course, her position was not helped by the fact that Nicholas who had known her since she was six years old, still saw her as a child. He would hardly listen to her advice even if he could bring himself to believe that she was old enough to offer any. As far as he was concerned she was little Lucy who had

started working for his uncle as soon as she left school
and would presumably continue to do so until the end of
the world. Nicholas had the great gift of endowing his
friends with eternal youth. Like Peter Pan and, of
course, himself, they were never allowed to grow up.

There was, thought Lucy wryly as she pushed open
the kitchen door and went inside, a certain irony in that.

She could hear the children's voices, high and excited,
somewhere in the distance. The kitchen itself was empty,
although the central table was full of pans and dishes that
looked as if they were ready to put into the oven. Lucy
had an instant vision of the latest incumbent of the
kitchen whom she had not yet met driven into headlong
flight by the children and hastened after the distant
voices.

They were in the snug. Nicholas, who liked to have the
log fire well alight by the time his first customer arrived,
had been in the middle of lighting it. The children were
always enchanted by the bellows and had begged to take
their turn. Nicholas agreed lightheartedly and by the
time Lucy arrived the children's exertions had produced
great roaring tongues of flame which filled the large
fireplace and disappeared, crackling ominously, up the
chimney. Nicholas watched uneasily.

'That's splendid, old chap,' he was assuring Boy. 'But
that's enough, don't you think?'

'But Angela hasn't had her second turn,' pointed out
Boy democratically.

Angela took the bellows enthusiastically.

'Couldn't you wait a bit?' hazarded Nicholas. 'I mean,
it dies down after a bit and gets awfully dull. It's much
more fun than when it's blazing like it is now.'

'We'll do it then *as well*,' Boy assured him.

Lucy came to his rescue. 'Angela, put those bellows down. Uncle Nicholas says you can do it later and so you can. But not now.'

Angela eyed her mutinously, lower lip beginning to pout. Nicholas was clearly relieved. However, he was also disastrously susceptible to brimming eyes. Quailing before Angela's reproachful demeanour, he was heard to murmur that perhaps a *little* blow wouldn't hurt.

All traces of tears disappeared. Triumphantly Angela turned back to the fire. She was intercepted.

'Angela,' said her aunt in a soft, dangerous voice.

She hesitated.

'I said, put those bellows down.'

'But Uncle Nicholas. . .'

'Doesn't want his chimney set on fire and his house burned down just to provide you with a little amusement,' stated Lucy with conviction.

Angela turned appealingly to Nicholas.

'Well, it's going very nicely now,' he said feebly. 'You don't want to overdo it. Why don't you both go and talk to Rusty? He's in the stable because he got out and he's filthy. You can brush him down if you like.'

Mollified, they went.

'Phew!' said Nicholas, mopping his brow dramatically. 'That child should go far. She has determination.'

'She's perfectly sensible if you explain to her properly,' said Lucy haughtily. 'It's very bad policy simply to give in to her every whim, though. That way she'll never find out that there are some things she can't have and some things that are dangerous to do.'

'It might be bad policy, but it's a damned sight easier,'

said Nicholas with feeling. 'I don't know how you control her. She just wouldn't take no for an answer.' He peered at Lucy. 'In fact you do look a bit under the weather. Those brats exhausted you?'

She chuckled. 'No, not really. I've been a bit behind-hand with the day ever since I got up. I was late at work and late at the bank and finally late at school. Oh, and I fell in the ditch,' she added, remembering her humiliation. 'Not a good day.'

'Poor love,' he said, taking her coat. 'Not that you're a good timekeeper at the best of times. I've spent more hours waiting at the bottom of the hill to take you into town on my crossbar than I have waiting for all the other women in my life put together.'

Lucy made a face. 'That was fifteen years ago,' she protested.

'You haven't changed,' he assured her blithely. 'Have a drink and drown your sorrows. Was there any particular reason for today's tardiness?'

Lucy accepted sherry, knowing she should be on the way home with the children but unwilling to forgo a few precious minutes with Nicholas. There had been a time when she would have plotted for days to win just as much of his attention as he was now giving her. Today she had stopped plotting just as she had stopped hoping that he would ever notice that she no longer had thin plaits bound with elastic bands and a gap between her front teeth. She had come, wryly, to expect nothing more and to hope for nothing more. It was enough that she enjoyed his confidence and his friendship. When Nicholas fell in love—and he fell in love frequently and vividly—it was with glamorous sophisticates. And, while Lucy might have hoped to convince him that she was no longer the inky-fingered little owl he remembered, she was sufficiently self-critical to know that she was not likely to achieve the degree of elegance which Nicholas demanded in his loves. She was therefore grateful for such fleeting interviews as these and content as long as her long-standing disregarded affection for him remained a secret.

'I've had things on my mind,' she said, answering him.

'Evidently,' he murmured, sitting down opposite her, smiling.

'I've had a letter from Peter,' she said abruptly.

'Peter?' He was startled. 'You mean your brother Peter?'

She nodded.

'I thought he was still in hospital. Are they going to let him out?'

'No.' She shook her head. 'I'm rather worried about that. It sounded as if he didn't think they were ever going to let him out.'

'*What?*'

She looked up quickly. 'He's been in hospital a year now. Ever since the floods in which Elaine was killed.'

'In Central America,' he nodded. 'I remember. That's when you got the children.'

'Yes. Well, he had some sort of fever—it sounded like malaria or something, but they said it was rare and he had to go to the States for treatment. He's been in the same hospital in San Francisco pretty well ever since. I suppose the company must be paying for it. Certainly it's the company that sends me the cheque for the children's keep every month. That's why Peter doesn't have to write. In the whole year he's only done so about three times—Christmas, the children's birthdays. . .' She broke off, biting her lip. 'And now I've had this long screed from him, rambling on about how the children need a father's guidance and how I'm too irresponsible to be left with them except as a temporary measure. I'm afraid he may want them to go to Elaine's parents.'

Nicholas shrugged. 'And that wouldn't be such a bad thing either. They could go to a decent school instead of this run-down bear-pit here, and it would leave you free to live your own life.'

'They *are* my life,' protested Lucy.

'Then they shouldn't be.'

'Oh, don't be obtuse. You know what I mean. They're part of my life. They won't cease to be part of it if they have to go to London and live with their grandparents.'

'Forget it,' he advised. 'It takes time to get things like that organised. He didn't actually tell you to dump them, did he?'

'N-no.'

'Then save the agonies till he does.' He stood up as the door to the snug opened. He swung round and a look half foolish, half extraordinarily touching came on to his face. Lucy gripped her hands together round the stem of her glass and tried not to mind. She had seen the look before. 'Lucy,' he said reverently. 'I don't think you've met Simone. She came in a package deal with the new chef.'

Lucy acknowledged satiny hair, great brown spaniel's eyes and as sweet a smile as she had seen on any of Nicholas's former loves. Her heart sank.

Simone was polite, but clearly her mind was elsewhere. She laid a soft hand on Nicholas's arm. 'There's a man outside who wants to know how early we start dinner. Apparently he's just moved into a house and has no kitchen yet, but he doesn't want to eat too late because he's got things to do. I said we could do it as soon as he liked. Is that all right?' She added ingenuously, 'He's super.'

'Do you think so?' Lucy repressed the urge to take Nicholas into a comforting cuddle. He stood looking very much like Boy when his father did not arrive at his birthday party, aggrieved, sorrowful and quite determined to put a brave face on it. Lucy swallowed. 'I think I know the man you must mean,' she offered. 'In fact it was he who drove me into the ditch, Nicholas. He seems to have moved into the old Manor—and not to think too highly of it, from the names he was calling it. Rather a shame, I thought. It's a beautiful house. But then he didn't really look the type to appreciate it.'

Simone protested charmingly, 'He is very attractive, Nicholas. I'm sure you will like him.'

'Do you think so?' he said doubtfully. 'Well, if he's to be a customer I shall have to like him, shan't I? God knows we could do with them.'

His expression wrung Lucy's heart. Unthinking, she tumbled into the fray on his behalf.

'Attractive? Surely not?' A door opened behind her, but as the hotel was not really open she paid no attention to it. It must be the children or the new chef or even the barman arriving for once before opening time. 'I thought,' said Lucy in her clearest, most precise little voice, 'that he looked distinctly scruffy.'

'You can't judge people by their clothes,' said Nicholas who, like her, had his back to the door.

'Well, I didn't like his expression,' she said firmly. 'He

was most unsympathetic when I fell down. And he looked—well, hard.'

Behind her there was a faint, devastating cough.

'I hope,' said the stranger humbly but with a wicked glint in his eye which he turned reproachfully on Lucy, 'you'll forgive this intrusion, but it was rather cold out there.' He had pulled a denim jacket over his wholly inadequate shirt, Lucy observed, and he was now huddling it round him melodramatically. 'I've been abroad a long time,' he explained, holding Lucy's eyes compellingly. 'I'd forgotten how—chilly—England can be.'

For one outraged moment she returned his mischievous look. Then, turning on her heel, she flounced out.

CHAPTER TWO

LUCY saw no more of the stranger at Windrush Manor in the next few weeks. Colonel Browning was trying to raise a sizeable loan to replace the Home Farm's ageing threshing machine and the work kept her fully occupied. She did not even have time to lend more than half an ear to Mrs Lamb's inexhaustible flow of information when she bought her groceries. The village was humming over the few scraps of fact that the new resident allowed to fall from time to time. Added to that was a good deal of speculation which was by far the more interesting.

Lucy gathered that the most widely held theory was that he was a long-lost descendant of old Mrs Appleton. 'Although Lamb thinks he's a spy—on account of them dark glasses and him carrying his passport around with him,' said Mrs Lamb disparagingly.

Absorbedly debating the merits of haddock—nourishing—or baked beans—infinitely more popular—for the children's tea, Lucy had only been half attending, but Mr Lamb's theory arrested her. She looked up, still clutching the box of frozen fish.

'A spy?' she echoed. 'One of ours, do you suppose? Or,' thrillingly, 'one of Theirs?'

Mrs Lamb looked blank for a moment and then laughed heartily. 'Go on with you, Lucy Wild! You're no better than Lamb with his silly ideas. It's all them trashy films on television that does it. What would a spy be

29

doing here, I ask you?'

Lucy considered it. 'He needn't be doing anything at the moment. He'd just be establishing his character. Then we'd get used to him and accept him as one of us. And *then*,' warming to her theme, 'some powerful politician or potty scientist or something would come and live here and then he could go to work, spying away like mad without anyone any the wiser.'

Mrs Lamb swallowed uneasily. 'Go on! A nice gentleman like that.'

'Oh, he'd have to be a nice gentleman,' Lucy assured her, 'or he'd never ingratiate himself properly. But I bet that's what he's here for. They call them,' she added carelessly, 'sleepers.' She held Mrs Lamb's disapproving gaze limpidly. 'Or perhaps he's from Whitehall. They must have heard that Colonel Browning has been looking at foreign threshers.'

Mrs Lamb snorted. 'You ought to be ashamed of yourself, Lucy. Making up such tales about respectable people!' She eyed her severely. 'And you've no call to stand there giggling. It's time you grew up. I don't know what those two mites are going to do for an example. For all you look so quiet and butter-wouldn't-melt-in-your-mouth, you're as great a madcap as you were at their age.'

'They don't seem to mind,' Lucy said mildly, deciding to be firm and make the children eat fish. She put it down on the counter with her other purchases.

Mrs Lamb ignored the gesture. 'I dare say they don't,' she sniffed. 'Wild by name and wild by nature—that's always been what's wrong with your family. I've seen them come and I've seen them go, and there hasn't been one died natural in his bed that I can recall.'

Lucy interrupted the familiar litany. 'You can hardly expect me to keep the children chained to the house because my grandfather broke his neck on the hunting field.'

'*And* your father, God rest him,' Mrs Lamb reminded her, dolorously adding up her bill.

'My father died in a road accident,' protested Lucy.

'Ah. Driving without proper care and attention was what they said, but going too fast was what they meant. It's a mercy he didn't take anyone else with him. He used to go racketing around with you and Peter sitting on his knee, till it fair made my blood run cold.'

'Well, there isn't room in my car for the children to sit on my knee,' said Lucy pacifically. She could not resent the strictures on her parent's style of driving, for they were kindly meant and were, in any case, basically justified.

'Just as well,' retorted Mrs Lamb. She accepted payment reluctantly. It was a dull afternoon and, once Lucy left, she would be unlikely to see another customer until the mothers ventured out to collect their children from school. Lucy looked rather anxiously at her watch. She had three letters to type and post before she could, with a clear conscience, go and meet Angela and Boy. So far she had done rather well about meeting them on time, but she knew that Miss Frobisher's eye was on her and any backsliding would be met with a severe reprimand. As Mrs Lamb slowly gave her her change she was already edging towards the door.

The curtain that hid the doorway into the little sitting-room behind the shop was pushed aside and Mr Lamb appeared at it, blinking after his afternoon nap.

'Here's Lamb,' cried his wife, triumphantly. 'Lamb, Lucy here agrees with you about Mr Challenger.'

He paused, bewildered.

Lucy said, 'Challenger?'

'That's his name,' said Mrs Lamb comfortably. 'Robert Challenger.'

'Leastways, that's what it's got on his cheques,' amended Mr Lamb portentously. '*I* didn't want to take his cheques. I said to Mother, I said—didn't I, Mother?—we don't know who he is nor where he's come from. All we know is, he's living up in the old manor. But that doesn't mean anything. But Mother wouldn't have it.'

'I said to Lamb—if he's a spy, which is a silly story and I don't for a moment believe, but *if* he is, then somebody will be paying his bills, even if he don't himself.'

'Oh, quite,' said Lucy, much entertained. 'They have their reputation to think of, after all.' She opened the door. 'I must get back to work. There's a lot to do and I daren't leave late or I won't be on time for the children. Goodbye.'

The Lambs looked after her regretfully.

'Hasn't a moment to herself, poor soul,' observed Mrs Lamb. 'She came running in here, just snatched up what she wanted and off again. No time for a bit of a chat. It's not like Lucy.'

'Well, I dare say she's got a lot to do, what with working for the Colonel and looking after those children.'

'It's not right,' said Mrs Lamb stoutly. 'It isn't even as if they were her own.'

'Ah, but she couldn't be fonder of them if they were.'

'I dare say, but that's not the point. They aren't hers, and Peter's got no right to saddle her with them.'

'He couldn't help being ill,' objected her husband. 'Nor he couldn't help his wife dying like that. And Lucy likes children.'

'And the rate she's going, she won't have any of her own,' snapped his wife.

He yawned hugely. 'Oh, I don't know. There's plenty of time for her to meet some young chap and settle down.'

'When?' demanded his wife. 'Where? There's nobody here in the village, and what time does she have to go anywhere else with those children at home? She wouldn't leave them on their own.'

Mr Lamb turned the proposition over in his mind. 'I don't see why she should have to go out and about to find herself a husband. You didn't.'

'The village was bigger then and all the young ones didn't go away to London. Who is there here now? Tell me that. Vicar?'

The Vicar was a widower of several years' standing who had hitherto resisted the attempts of his faithful parish to see him married again. Mr Lamb chuckled.

'No, I don't say as the Vicar'd do for Lucy Wild. But there's others.'

'Who?' snapped his wife.

'Well, now. What about Nicholas at the Royal Oak?'

She snorted. 'That flibbertigibbet! She's too sensible to take him.'

'Oh.' He scratched the side of his nose thoughtfully.

Then he said with caution, 'I did think as young Lucy was rather fond of him.'

'Of course she's fond of him. She's known him all her life. Doesn't mean she'll marry him. If she was going to she'd have done it by now.'

Mr Lamb subsided. 'Oh!'

Mrs Lamb nodded sadly. 'And she's not getting any younger.'

'Well, what about this new chap up at the Manor?' he said, inspired. 'He might do—if he isn't a foreign agent, that is.'

His wife looked at him scornfully. 'From what I know of that family,' she said, 'he'll only do if he is.'

It was not only the Lambs who were interested in the new arrival, as Lucy found on her return to the Home Farm. Mrs Browning, in her own dignified and ladylike way, had put Mr Challenger under review.

'Collecting a damned dossier on the fellow,' was how her husband put it.

Lucy found him sitting in the window seat of the fine old library, looking worried.

'Adelaide wants you,' he greeted her. 'Some charity thing. Better leave those letters till tomorrow now.'

She protested.

'No, no, much better leave them. Then I can have a good think after dinner this evening. You go off to Adelaide—she's in her sitting-room. She got some plan for Windrush Manor, so she's been snooping.' He brooded. 'God knows what she's up to. She was burbling about a dance. A *dance*!' he repeated with loathing.

'At the Manor?' said Lucy, startled.

'Precisely. Heaven knows how she'll manage it. I

mean, one can't go bang up to a perfect stranger and ask if one can hold a dance in his house.'

'One can if it's for charity,' said Lucy in a pale voice. She had assisted Mrs Browning before in her energetic fund-raising programmes and was not anxious to repeat the experience.

'Charity! Fiddlesticks. A lot of women without enough to do sticking their noses in where they're not wanted,' said the Colonel, a man of strong prejudices. 'Serve 'em right if the fellow kicks them out. Will he, do you suppose?' he added hopefully.

Lucy sighed sympathetically. As she well knew, Adelaide Browning's charitable activities usually resulted at some point in the Colonel climbing into his musty tails, protesting hotly but vainly, and patronising whatever function was involved. The functions themselves were of uniform inferiority and would have been dull but for the disasters which invariably struck them. Lucy, on the whole, rather enjoyed the whole thing once the committee meetings were disposed of and the practical arrangements safely delegated—again an invariable feature of Mrs Browning's campaigns—into her own capable hands. Colonel Browning, a bluff, amiable man with a horror of appearing conspicuous, loathed them. His wife inevitably cast him as patron of her various causes which entailed him making speeches and presenting prizes. Nevertheless it was still easier to accede to his wife's requests for participation than to rebel. Lucy could well understand his hoping that Challenger might be made of sterner stuff.

'I don't know much about him,' she said thoughtfully. 'I've only met him once and he seemed—er—very self-assured. I wouldn't have thought Mrs Browning would persuade him to have a dance unless he wanted one. On the other hand, he might think it was a good idea—to open the house and introduce himself to the local people. I don't know.'

'Adelaide does,' he said gloomily. 'She's compiled a damned dossier on the fellow. Oh, go away and learn the worst. God help us if the poor devil gives in.'

But so far was the elusive Mr Challenger from succumbing to Mrs Browning's undeniable powers of persuasion that he had not so far even accepted one of her pressing invitations to drinks, dinner or—a desperate throw, this last—tea. He was very sorry, it was very kind of her, but he was very busy and too unsure of his movements to say with any certainty when he would be free.

'At least, that's what he *says*,' complained Adelaide Browning, pouring out her woes to Lucy. 'I think he's avoiding me.'

'Oh, surely not,' she protested, adding, rather undiplomatically, 'He's not been here long enough. . .'

'To find out that I always want something when I ask people to dinner?' suggested Adelaide, quite unoffended. 'No, I wouldn't have thought he'd been here long enough either. Perhaps,' she added darkly, 'Tom has been having words with him behind my back.'

Lucy chuckled. 'Or perhaps he's just naturally wary?'

Adelaide flung up her hands. 'In that case, God help us. We'll never get the Manor if he is.'

'Er—what do you want the Manor *for*?' asked Lucy, hoping she did not know the answer.

Adelaide wriggled down among the cushions in the

window seat of her pretty sitting-room and looked smug. 'I'm glad you asked me that,' she said. 'It's rather a pet scheme of mine. Pour yourself some coffee and come and sit down. It's in the hearth. I only made it a few minutes ago.'

Lucy did as she was bid with a surreptitious glance at her watch.

'Very well, tell me everything,' she said resignedly. 'I don't seem to have any more work to do for Colonel Browning this afternoon. But I warn you, I must leave on the dot of twenty past three or I shall be late.'

'Oh, the children,' said Adelaide vaguely. 'Dont worry about them. I'll run you down in the car. It'll be worth it,' she added reflectively, 'to hold on to you. You're my only sympathetic audience. Everyone else is bored with me. And Tom, poor darling, keeps hoping I'll lose heart and give up. But I shan't.'

Lucy could believe it. 'Give up what?' she asked, clearing a pile of papers from a brocade chair and sitting down in it gingerly. She took a sip of her coffee and looked at Adelaide expectantly.

'My Jacobean evening,' said that lady thrillingly.

'Your——?' Lucy boggled. '*Jacobean?*'

Adelaide nodded triumphantly.

'But—how?' Lucy thought for a moment and then added, 'Why?'

'Why? The Roman Way, of course,' said Adelaide, looking pained. 'Why else?'

Lucy blinked. This oblique utterance did not confuse her entirely, for she was aware of Mrs Browning's enthusiastic championing of the old Roman road which ran along the hills. It was an ancient right of way which

had long since fallen into disuse until one of the larger
properties had been left to the National Trust, which had
promptly restored the footpath and opened as much of it
as lay across public land to wayfarers. There remained
only a brief stretch of a mile or so between the National
Trust land and a much frequented bridle path where the
old road lay across cultivated fields. Mrs Browning's
committee had been formed with the purpose of raising
the finance to buy the three relevant fields and present
them to the nation, once the County Council had
established that the right of way had not been made use
of for so long that it had ceased to apply.

Lucy had written all the letters and seen most of the
councillors involved, so she understood Mrs Browning's
remark. But she was puzzled.

'A Jacobean evening?' she echoed. 'But what was
special about the Jacobeans? Why not a Roman evening,
if there has to be one?'

'Because we haven't got a Roman villa in the village
and we have got a Jacobean one,' snapped Adelaide. She
was disappointed in Lucy's reaction. 'Windrush Manor
is perfect—especially the garden. Though I suppose we
can't use the garden in winter and I did want this to come
off soon.'

'Soon?' said Lucy with a sense of foreboding. Mrs
Browning was inclined to be impatient of delay in
realising her plans, which accounted in no small measure
for the frequency of the disasters which attended her
projects. Therefore, 'How soon?' she demanded.

Adelaide was airy. 'Oh, in time for Christmas.'

Lucy swallowed.

The other regarded her severely. 'You don't want to

leave these things hanging in the air,' she said largely. 'They go stale.'

'But—*Christmas*,' murmured Lucy in a hollow voice.

'Of course. We can have great log fires and the dramatic society can do something from *Twelfth Night*. The children can sing carols and you can play that thing of yours——' Lucy was the owner of a much cherished lute which, as Adelaide Browning knew very well, she constantly refused to play in public '—and we can roast an ox. . .'

Lucy rose from her seat. 'No,' she said with quiet force.

'But naturally, dear. Nicholas can deal with it,' returned Adelaide, as one making concessions.

Lucy stood firm. 'No ox,' she said.

Adelaide was injured. 'But why ever not? If Nicholas doesn't mind cooking it.'

'Nicholas,' said Lucy grimly, for she knew her beloved as well as she knew his aunt and her fondness for both of them could not disguise what painful experience had taught her, 'won't be buying the beast, and transporting it and seeing that it's cleaned and that there's a spit long enough and a fire big enough——' She tailed off, quite overcome by horrid visions.

'But it would be so splendid,' wheedled Adelaide. 'We could have a bonfire down by the river and——'

'No bonfire. No ox.' Lucy looked her straight in the eye. 'Not if you want me to organise it.'

'Well, of course, I don't want you to *organise*,' protested the ruffled lady. 'I know that would be too great a responsibility for you, dear. And when would you have the time, working for Tom as you do and looking after the children every evening? No, I can see that I shall have to *organise* it all myself, as I always do. Nobody ever has time to help other people nowadays. I never thought you'd be able to take on a great deal, but I *did* think you might take a *little* off my hands. Fetching and carrying, running a few errands—nothing that would put you out, of course. None of the tiresome committee work. But I had hoped I might be able to delegate a little of the *practical* side to you.' She sighed. Her tone said that the practical side was as nothing compared with her own bravely borne burden.

Shaken but resolved, Lucy stood her ground. 'No ox,' she said.

Unexpectedly, Mrs Browning gave way. 'Oh, very well,' she said pettishly. 'Though I think you're very unromantic.'

Lucy acknowledged the justice of the accusation ruefully. 'I always have been, I think,' she reflected.

'So different from Nicholas,' mourned his aunt. 'Now he said at once what a lovely scheme it was. *He* didn't make stupid objections about spits and things.'

'He wouldn't,' said Lucy with irony.

It went unobserved. 'No,' agreed his aunt. 'He has more imagination than most people.'

Lucy assented to the hypothesis unemotionally.

'Anyway, the whole question is academic at the moment,' she pointed out after a pause. 'As far as I can see you haven't yet been able to track down Mr Challenger and ask his permission. Until you do, there's not much point in doing anything else.'

'Aha! You think he'll say no,' said Adelaide acutely.

Lucy grinned. 'Not precisely,' she deprecated.

'You think he'll put me off?'

Lucy, who suspected that Mr Challenger's evasive tactics were not wholly fortuitous, was fairly sure that Mrs Browning would not be offered an opportunity to expound her magnificent scheme for his house to him. She wondered idly who his benefactor might be. Clearly he had a friend and had had warning about Mrs Browning's persistence in pursuit of her charitable ends.

'Not quite that, perhaps,' she murmured. 'But after all, he doesn't seem to work here, does he? He may just have bought the house for holidays or weekends or something. I don't think you should count on seeing him and getting him to agree.'

'If I can get hold of him, he'll agree,' said Adelaide confidently. She looked at her watch. 'In fact I'll go and see him this evening after I've taken you home. It's time we were going. Come on.'

All the way to the school she continued to talk about her idea. On the way back to Hazel Cottage she expounded to the children her plans for them to participate, which fascinated them. By the time Mrs Browning's Mini disappeared in the direction of Windrush Manor Angela was planning to let her hair grow, for, as she solemnly told Lucy, if they performed a nativity play as Mrs Browning wanted them to, she would insist on being the Angel of the Lord. And whoever heard of an angel with short hair?

Lucy, forseeing stormier waters ahead than she had at first envisaged, sighed and agreed.

Boy's plans for his debut were less impressive than Angela's but none the less fraught with danger. Boy could see himself as a shepherd.

'Oh, yes?' said Lucy a little absently, as she brushed Angela's hair. 'That will be nice.'

'And I can borrow Billy Marshall's Daft Willy,' he said cheerfully.

The Marshalls were farmers who had allowed, during the lambing season, their youngest son to adopt the smallest bottle-fed lamb. By autumn it was a full grown foolish animal, firmly convinced that its rightful place was indoors with people. It accompanied Billy on his frequent visits to Hazel Cottage and Lucy had come to regard it philosophically. But she had not imagined that the creature would be introduced into Windrush Manor under Boy's patronage when she did so.

She tried to hide her dismay. 'You mean a shepherd with sheep?' she queried faintly.

Boy nodded.

'That's very—original.' She paused, gave Angela's hair a final brush and turned the little girl round. 'But surely the shepherds left their flocks behind them?'

'I wouldn't have done,' said Boy stoutly.

'That is unanswerable,' acknowledged his aunt. 'I suppose we shall just have to see what happens.' She looked from one to the other of them and then said in a neutral voice, 'Of course Mrs Browning's plans aren't always quite—quite *reliable*. Very often she intends to do something—really, really means to—and circumstances prevent her. You must try to remember that, and not be too disappointed if it doesn't come off.'

They looked at her in silent reproach.

'I mean, there's always the nativity play in church.'

'That's for babies,' said Angela dismissingly.

'And Vicar won't let us have real animals. It's just silly

dressing up,' objected Boy.

'I see your point,' admitted Lucy. 'But——' She stopped abruptly. She had been unbuttoning Angela's dressing gown before installing her in bed and found her nightdress was not properly fastened at the neck, showing the edge of a vicious bruise. Pushing the material gently aside, she saw the extent of the ugly mark. She looked at Angela severely. 'What's that?'

Angela hung her head. Boy shuffled uncomfortably.

'Well?'

Silence.

'Angela, did you hear me? How did you get this bruise? Did,' with horrid vision of playground bullies, 'someone push you over?'

Angela still said nothing, but Boy seemed pleased to be asked a question he could answer with unhelpful truth.

'Not *someone*,' he demurred.

Angela glared at him.

Lucy frowned. '*Not* someone? Then what? Surely not a car? Nobody would knock a child over and not tell. One of Colonel Browning' cows,' she hazarded, inspired.

Angela shook her head dumbly.

'Well then?' They stared at her with their own peculiar deprecating mulishness which she found both touching and impossible to deal with. She sat back on her heels, regarding them both a little helplessly. Boy began to scratch one foot down the back of the other leg. He avoided her eye. Not for the first time she wondered if their real mother would have had the same difficulties with them as she occasionally found, and her brow creased worriedly.

'Be sensible,' she pleaded. 'Whatever it is, I won't be

angry if you tell me the truth.'

'Well,' said Boy reluctantly, 'it was a picture.'

She sat down on the carpet in her surprise. 'A *picture*? At school? What sort of picture?'

Boy looked at Angela, who was twisting her hands together and showed every sign of dissolving into tears any moment. 'Not at school. It was——' He swallowed and went on bravely, 'It was up at the old house.'

Lucy looked from one child to the other, bewildered. 'What old house?' she demanded.

Angela spoke for the first time. 'The man's.' Lucy drew a long unsteady breath and she added swiftly, 'You said you wouldn't be angry.'

The breath was expelled on a long sigh. 'So I did,' said Lucy with admirable self-control. 'I gather you've been visiting Windrush Manor. You'd better tell me all about it.'

Nothing loath, now that the first confession was out of the way, they sat down beside her on the bedroom rug and launched into their narrative. It was very simple and, to Lucy, quite appalling.

They had been intrigued by the stranger as soon as they met him and their curiosity had not abated with the weeks. At school their stock had soared when Angela had casually let it fall that they had actually ridden in his car. This had prompted her to suggest to Boy that, in order to maintain their new prestige, it might be a good plan to pursue the acquaintance.

Accordingly they had, on their weekend outings with Rusty, ventured up to the Manor. There was nothing in itself unusual in this. In common with all the other village children they were in the habit of regarding both the Home Wood and the Manor orchard as licensed playgrounds. But they would not normally have gone as far as the house. Nor would they have tried to go inside. Mr Challenger, encountering two muddy children with an enormous and equally dirty dog on his doorstep, had not been best pleased. He had told them to go and play elsewhere with just that degree of impatient superiority guaranteed to provoke an independent spirit like Boy's.

The ensuing weeks had been enlivened by a succession of secret sorties into forbidden territory. They had found a way into the house through a french window with a faulty catch. Just at first Angela had held back, but as they were never caught and never disturbed they had both grown braver and ventured beyond the old drawing-room upstairs into the attic rooms where the Jacobean servants had slept and which were now stuffed full of intriguing rubbish.

For the first time Angela became enthusiastic in her tale. Clearly she had enjoyed the attics.

'And was that where the picture fell on you?' said Lucy patiently.

Apparently not. The picture had fallen on Angela that very day. The whole school had gone on a nature walk and Boy and Angela, interpreting their brief rather liberally, had made for the Manor. A good deal had seemed to be going on at the front door. There were large vans drawn up in the drive and a good deal of coming and going between them and the house. The children had still reckoned their secret entrance to be safe enough, however, particularly as there was no sign of the man, as Angela explained innocently, and had entered by the drawing-room window as usual—only to find that a

number of pieces of furniture had been stored in the
hitherto half-empty room. In particular some large
paintings of the sea had been propped up against the
window which their surreptitious entrance disturbed.
They managed to get in all right, but in doing so they
dislodged the paintings which had fallen with a resounding crash. They had fled, but not before one of them had
caught Angela a painful blow on the shoulder.

Lucy patted the affected area absentmindedly. 'Did
anyone see you?' she said with that grasp of essentials
which the children particularly admired in her.

Angela, who had brightened during the telling, looked
ready to cry again, which her brother was quick to
explain.

'She squawked,' he said disgustedly. 'Otherwise they
wouldn't have known we were there. But when the
picture fell on her she gave a great squawk and they came
in and caught us.'

'Oh, dear!' Lucy thought. 'I suppose they didn't ask
your names?'

Angela crept closer in the circle of her arm.

'Well, not exactly,' allowed Boy. 'But they asked us
what we were doing and we said we were on a nature
walk. And they said,' he finished miserably, 'that they
would see Miss Frobisher.'

'Oh, *dear*!' said Lucy with feeling. 'And we aren't too
popular with Miss Frobisher anyway. Oh, well, I
suppose it can't be helped. Did you notice if there was
any damage to the picture at all?'

'We couldn't lift it,' volunteered Angela, rubbing a
forefinger round her eyes. 'We were going to stand it up
again,' she explained, 'and pretend we'd never been

there. Only it was too heavy.'

Lucy frowned worriedly. 'In that case it might have hurt you badly.' She inspected the bruise closely but could see no signs of undue discolouration or that her gentle proddings caused Angela to wince more than she would have expected. 'Can you move your arm?'

Angela swung her arms energetically, windmill-fashion.

'Yes, I can see you can,' said Lucy, not quite dodging in time. Her hair was sent flying wildly by a glancing blow. She shook it out of her eyes. 'Does your shoulder hurt? Is it stiff?'

Again Angela experimented.

'Only when I press it,' she decided at last, suiting her action to words and wincing dramatically.

'Then you'd best go to bed now,' said Lucy, 'and we'll see how it is in the morning. If it hurts, we'll go to Dr Fraser. But for now—bed.'

Nothing loath, Angela scrambled off the hearthrug and into bed among an impressive row of stuffed animals. Her favourite was a rather battered panda with uneven eyes, as he had lost one on a trip to London and had to have it replaced by one of a different shade which was all Lucy's button box had to offer. Angela, a philosophical child, said it made him special and loved him all the more. Nevertheless, Lucy knew that she felt he was not quite as beautiful as before and therefore always now allotted him pride of place in her nursery menagerie so that he should not feel hurt. Lucy annually knitted him waistcoats and made him nightshirts that matched Angela's own nightdresses for the same reason.

Panda was now therefore solemnly taken out of his cherry-red waistcoat and put into night attire and then tucked in beside Angela. Boy and Lucy kissed them both goodnight and Boy went to his own room. Lucy lit the nightlight, put it on top of the wardrobe so it should not shine in Angela's eyes, and left quietly. In five minutes, she knew, Angela would be fast asleep.

Not so Boy. He went to bed every evening surrounded by paper and crayons and all manner of necessary flotsam with which he announced himself to be drawing. He then fell asleep in stages. Lucy usually found herself picking acorns or bits of bark off his eiderdown and drawing the bedcovers up about his ears when she went to bed herself. And changing his sheets regularly produced a shower of pencils that had been lost during his artistic activities.

Tonight, however, he did not want to draw but went straight to bed with uncharacteristic quietness.

'Do you want some hot chocolate?' asked Lucy, concerned.

He turned over with his back to her and locked his arms round his knees. He shook his head.

'Are you sure?' she persisted.

Again a silent headshake.

'Very well.' She went to the door, after brushing his averted cheek with her lips. 'Do you want me to leave the door open?'

Boy had long since given up nightlights, but he did have occasional bouts of disliking the dark.

'No, thank you,' he said politely.

'All right,' said Lucy, feeling helpless again and rather worried. 'But call out if you want anything.'

She went downstairs thoughtfully. Boy had obviously
got a guilty conscience because he had led Angela into an
escapade which looked as if it might have dire reper-
cussions for them all. Angela was still at the age when
she could find release in confession and a hearty bout
of tears, but Boy was sufficiently grown up to realise
that 'I'm sorry' was not the magical panacea that his
sister supposed it to be. Lucy remembered making that
painful discovery for herself and sympathised. She hoped
he was not really fearful of retribution. Of course, they
had been naughty, but as far as she could see they had
done no real damage. She could not really imagine the
man she had met filled with righteous wrath at the
children's adventures. If it had been the Colonel now,
who thought that children, like puppies, should stay out
of doors where they could do no harm, the case would be
very different. Or even the Vicar, though he conscien-
tiously tried to enter into the pastimes of his younger
congregation, might have taken the occasion to deliver a
few grave words on the subject of respecting other
people's property. But Challenger——! Lucy tried to
imagine that particular man delivering a lecture to the
children and giggled. He had far more the appearance of
one who would show them how not to get caught next
time.

She switched on the table lamp and settled down with
the accumulated tears, scuffs and wrenched seams of the
children's weekly washing. She was still busy congratu-
lating herself that she need not expect a visit from an irate
householder, with one ear open for sounds of distress
from the children's rooms, when she was startled by a
resounding knock at the door.

Puzzled, she pushed aside her workbasket and went to open it.

On her doorstep, wet and windswept and clearly furious, stood Robert Challenger.

'Oh,' said Lucy in a pale voice, her hand falling from the door. She cast a nervous look up the stairs, but as far as she could see Boy's door remained firmly shut. She squared her shoulders. Obviously the man was going to be unpleasant and she must do her best to shield the children from what was, equally obviously, a far from sweet temper. She swallowed. 'You'd better come in.'

Almost furtively she shepherded him round the staircase and out of earshot of the children, firmly closing the sitting-room door behind him.

'I——' he began, but she hushed him unceremoniously until she had closed the door.

He watched her, an arrested expression on his face. Anger gave way to that deplorably superior amusement she had seen before.

'Enemy active tonight?' he said in a stage whisper, his mouth solemn.

Lucy looked at him with dislike. 'I just don't want to disturb the children,' she said softly.

He was taken aback. 'Er—no, I suppose not,' he whispered back. 'Do you think it would disturb them if we talked normally? This muttering is very painful on the larynx.'

'Of course,' said Lucy with disdain, in her ordinary voice. 'It doesn't matter now the door's shut. I just didn't want to let Boy hear you if he should happen to be awake.'

His eyebrows flew up. 'Boy?'

'My nephew,' explained Lucy. She sat down on the arm of a shabby chair and sighed. 'You have met,' she added sadly.

'Oh, yes, so we have.' He did not seem disposed to continue the subject but stood looking down at her, half-smiling. 'Doesn't he like you having callers after dark?'

She snorted. 'Don't be flippant. The poor child's been in an absolute fever waiting for you to turn up all day.' It was an exaggeration, but it was a subject on which she felt strongly.

'Has he?' he said, fascinated. 'How very perspicacious of him. Tell me, does he have second sight? Or is he the little monster who scatters broken milk bottles in the road to rip up the tyres of the unwary traveller?'

'He's *not* a little monster,' she fired up. 'He's just an ordinary mischievous child and—*what* did you say?'

His mouth twitched. 'Milk bottles,' he said gently. 'Broken milk bottles. They're strewn all over the road out there, with the result that my car has not one but three flat tyres. I wanted to use your telephone if I might.'

'Oh,' she said weakly. She could see, now that she looked, that his fingers were covered in black grease. He must have changed, or begun to change, one tyre before he discovered the state of the others. That would account for the expression of black fury on his face. A treacherous desire to laugh rose in her, but she sternly suppressed it. 'Of—of course,' she said, only the slightest tremor in her voice. She indicated the telephone on a bookcase in the corner of the room. 'Over there. If you want the garage in the village the number's on the pad.'

He looked at her narrowly.

'I'll—I'll make you some coffee while you're phoning,' she gasped. 'I'm sure you're wet and cold.'

And escaping to the kitchen she gave way to a paroxysm of mirth.

She was wiping her eyes on a convenient drying-up cloth when she became aware of being watched. Robert Challenger was standing ominously in the doorway. From his attitude, one arm negligently on the frame above his head, one foot crossed in front of the other, she inferred he had been there for several seconds, and therefore had witnessed her unseemly fit of the giggles. Still choking intermittently on a nervous laugh, she gave a final defiant wipe to her eyes and faced him.

'Do you always laugh so immoderately at other people's disasters?' he demanded, surveying her.

She hiccuped. 'N-not invariably.'

'I think you must be mad,' he said, as one making a discovery. 'First of all you spirit me into the house as if it were being watched by the Special Branch. Then you claim your nephew has foretold my coming and now I find you having hysterics in the kitchen.'

She chuckled. 'I'm sorry. It must look strange, I know. . .'

'It does,' he assured her. 'At least to me. But then I'm a comparative newcomer. A good deal of what goes on in this village seems strange to me. I'm not sure I shall survive the pace of rural life. The people in the little shop clearly suspect me of dark doings up at Dracula's Palace. . .'

Lucy giggled again at his unflattering reference to his house.

He went on, ignoring her, 'Both the Colonel's lady and

the Vicar track me down remorselessly—why, I can't imagine. There's you, who are clearly unhinged. And today my house was invaded by some lethal tots who did their best to demolish the only decent painting in the place.'

'How—how unfortunate,' said Lucy airily.

He looked at her suspiciously.

'Was it very valuable?' she added hastily, not quite keeping the anxiety out of her voice.

His eyes widened in comprehension. 'I *see*,' he said softly. '*Your* lethal tots.'

For a craven moment Lucy was tempted to deny it. After all, if he wasn't sure and had no proof, he could hardly persecute the children. Only the thought of explaining her dissimulation to Boy prevented her. Her nephew's uncomfortable conscience extended to his immediate family, and he was at the age to be very severe with Lucy's evasions. She stopped laughing and hung her head.

'I'm afraid so,' she agreed. 'Was the painting very valuable? I do hope they didn't do any irreparable damage. From what Boy told me, I thought they'd come off rather the worse in the encounter.'

He frowned quickly. 'You mean the child was hurt?'

'Angela was a little. That's how I found out. She couldn't explain the bruise away, so I made her tell me the truth. It doesn't look as if it's much.'

'Has she seen a doctor?'

'I hardly think. . .'

'I can well believe it,' he said unkindly. 'For heaven's sake, woman, that painting had been in the attic for a hundred years or more. God knows what bugs it carried.'

Lucy eyed him with hostility. 'I am well aware of the dangers,' she said frostily. 'However, I don't lose my head every time one of the children bumps his knee. Angela had a bruise, but the picture hadn't broken the skin. Therefore she has a sore shoulder and a good fright, neither of which is likely to prove fatal. What I'm more interested in is the damage to your picture. You must of course allow me to pay for it.'

He dismissed it. 'That's nonsense.'

'I,' said Lucy militantly, 'insist.'

He began to look harassed. 'Well, I don't know how much it will cost, or even if I can find anyone to repair it.'

Lucy subsided, torn between guilt and an obscure feeling of dissatisfaction with the man. It was as if he did not take her seriously. He might be joking when he said she was mad, but he had not been laughing when he berated her for not taking Angela instantly to the doctor. What business was it of his? she thought resentfully. Yet one did not like to appear foolishly irresponsible in anybody's eyes, even those of a worldly and indifferent stranger.

'Well, if you can find someone to do it, you must send the bill to me,' she pursued, rather sulkily.

He sighed. 'Oh, very well. And now please may I wash my hands?'

'What?' She stared at him nonplussed. He waved grimy hands under her nose and she took a step backwards. 'Oh! Of course.'

'Then perhaps I can telephone the garage to come and collect my car. At present it's lurching drunkenly up against your hedge.'

Lucy gave him soap and a towel without comment.
'Thank you.'

He went back into the sitting-room and she heard him talking on the telephone while she filled the ancient percolator and set it on the stove. When he returned to the kitchen there was a delicious smell of coffee.

He did not appear to appreciate it. 'The old fool says the car will have to stay there till morning.'

'I thought he would,' said Lucy serenely, putting mugs on a tray. 'Are you hungry?'

'Yes. What do you mean you thought he would? Why didn't you say so?'

'Because I wasn't sure. And anyway, he might have come out for you. He won't for me. He's a curmudgeonly soul and he doesn't approve of women drivers. So it's a sort of triumph for him when my car breaks down.'

'He doesn't approve of foreign sports cars either,' he said ruefully. 'Or the people who drive them.'

'Oh, well,' said Lucy philosophically. 'It could be worse. When you've finished I'll get the car out and drive you back to the Manor. How hungry are you? Cheese sandwich hungry or do you want a proper fry-up?'

He looked at her in amazement. 'Are you proposing to feed me?'

For some unaccountable reason Lucy blushed. 'Well, you're wet and cold,' she said gruffly. 'It's a horrible night.'

'It is indeed.' He took the tray from her as she began to butter large slices of crusty bread. 'And not made any better, I imagine, by me stamping in here and—er—disturbing the children. This is very charitable of you.'

'I'd do the same for anybody,' Lucy assured him

untruthfully, conveniently forgetting Jane Frobisher and the Howards from the garage. 'If the truth is known it's probably my milk bottle that's the cause of the trouble. We put them in the hedge so the milkman doesn't have to come all the way up to the house to deliver, but it's not really satisfactory. I think one must have rolled out tonight—there's a strong wind up. I'd better go and brush the pieces out of the road before somebody else comes to grief.'

She put the plate of sandwiches on the tray and said, 'Go and sit by the fire and have your coffee. It won't take a minute.'

He handed the tray back to her, laughing. 'I hope not. But it won't take *me* a minute. I'm dressed for the weather.'

He took the broom from her resistless hand and marched to the front door. Inside five minutes he was back, taking off his thick duffle coat and clapping his hands together to bring the blood back into them. Lucy drew a stout old chair to the fire for him and poured steaming coffee into a mug.

'There you are,' she said as she would have done to Boy or Angela. 'You shouldn't have gone out again. You've probably caught pneumonia or something. And it was almost certainly my fault that the horrid thing smashed anyway. What with your car and your painting I seem to put a jinx on your possessions.'

He made deprecating noises through a mouthful of cheese sandwich.

'And you've been very considerate,' she continued, determined to be diplomatic. 'About the children and everything. I'm rather deeply in your debt.'

She gave him what she hoped was an appealing look. He would disclaim and then she would ask him to forgive the children. But her policy proved vain.

He returned her look quizzically.

'Yes, you are, aren't you?' he agreed.

CHAPTER THREE

THERE was a stunned silence while Lucy tried to think of a dignified retort. At last she abandoned the attempt.

'There's no need to sound so *pleased* about it,' she said crossly. 'Anyone would think you welcomed having your goods and chattels destroyed.'

He considered it, eyes half-closed. 'No, I don't think I would say that,' he demurred. 'Not *welcomed* exactly. But I am not altogether opposed to having you in my debt.'

Lucy eyed him suspiciously. The remark sounded faintly threatening in some way which she did not choose to explore.

'Why?' she demanded.

He seemed to be debating his reply. He stretched comfortably in the old chair, sinking deeper into its battered cushions and letting his eyelids droop until Lucy began to wonder seriously whether he was falling asleep under the combined influences of the warm fire and her awkward questions.

When he eventually spoke, it was irrelevantly. 'This is a remarkably pleasant room,' he murmured.

'Thank you,' she said, sitting a little straighter in her chair and fixing him with an imperative eye. '*Why* do you want me in your debt?'

His eyelids lifted and he smiled at her lazily. 'As a sort of tactical move,' he explained with a great air of frankness.

'Tactical?' Lucy was now utterly lost. 'I wish,' she said roundly, 'you'd stop making oblique threats and tell me whatever it is.'

He sighed. 'And I was so comfortable. I warn you, you won't like it. Will you throw me out the moment I've finished and never let me darken your door again?'

He looked so comically anxious, clutching a coffee mug protectively to his shirt front, that Lucy found her errant sense of humour betrayed her again. She began to laugh.

'Very probably,' she agreed. 'Do you want indemnity before you begin? Very well,' she said as she had said to Boy earlier that evening, 'if you tell me the truth, I won't be angry with you.'

'Ah, but can I rely on that?' he murmured provocatively.

'I would think so,' she retorted. 'If the children fail to induce me to lose my temper and break my promises of forbearance then I shouldn't think you could do so.'

'A comforting thought,' he said ironically.

He put his cup down but, in spite of the fact that he was smiling, she thought she could still detect the vestiges of several less pleasant expressions in his face. His mouth had taken a rather hard line and she suspected that, behind the dark lenses, his eyes were grim. She quelled a flutter of nervousness and folded her hands in her lap.

'First of all, I'd better introduce myself.'

She looked blankly at him. 'But I know your name,' she pointed out.

His mouth relaxed. 'And that's enough?' he asked, amused.

She nodded. 'Unless you want to show me your driving licence or your police badge or something,' she added, remembering Mr Lamb's flights of fancy.

'My *what*?'

'Or your CIA identity card,' she expanded, and began to laugh at his expression.

'You *are* mad,' he said with great calm. 'I knew you were.'

'No, no. Or if I am, it's a madness many a respectable man shares. Well,' she added fairly, 'one respectable man.' She giggled helplessly while he watched her with ostentatious patience. 'I'm sorry.' She wiped her eyes. 'You see, Mr Lamb—you know, Mr Lamb at the village shop—will have it that you're not what you seem. He thinks you're a secret agent but hasn't made up his mind which side you're on.'

His face relaxed and he laughed softly. 'And you plumped for the CIA. Why?'

'Ah, well,' began Lucy enjoyably, 'when you first arrived it didn't look to me as if you'd just flown in from the frozen wastes of Russia. Not the way you were dressed. Hence the CIA.' She sat back, pleased with herself.

His mouth twitched. 'Chopped logic, my child. I could have been spying for the KGB in the West Indies. You shouldn't judge by appearances.'

'I didn't think of that,' said Lucy, crestfallen.

'You will next time,' he said kindly. 'Is there any more coffee?'

She picked up the percolator and swirled it experimentally. 'I don't know how hot it is,' she warned, filling the mug he held out to her. 'Did you really come here to confess that you're an international spy?' she asked, interested.

'Would you believe me, if I said yes?'

She pondered. 'I wouldn't have any reason to disbelieve you,' she opined. 'So yes, I dare say I would.'

He surveyed her, half-smiling. 'You tempt me, you really do. But I cannot tell a lie to such trusting innocence. I'm a mere engineer, quite ordinary and unexciting.'

Lucy thought of the reaction to his arrival in the village and suppressed a chuckle, contenting herself with a modest, 'I wouldn't say that.'

'Oh, I assure you. I spend most of my days closeted with a drawing board and a slide rule.'

'And the West Indies?' murmured Lucy.

'I'd been building a bridge there,' he acknowledged. 'What a little sleuth you are!'

'Bridges?' Her head jerked up. 'But that's what my brother does. He works for a big contractor, though, he's not freelance.'

'We call them consultants,' he said primly. 'Yes, I know about Peter. I've——'

'Met him?'

'Worked with him,' he corrected. 'In fact I worked with him in Honduras. I even stayed with him and Elaine before the floods in which she died.'

'*Did* you?' Lucy was more bewildered than ever. 'But why didn't you say so at once? And what coincidence brought you here. . .?' Her voice trailed off. 'It wasn't coincidence, was it?' she said quietly.

'I'm afraid not.'

She stood up and went to the window, staring out

unseeingly into the dark garden with the darker lane
beyond. Dimly she could see a faint glow which she
supposed must be the lights of his car. She wrapped her
arms across her body, surprised to feel the coldness of
her own hands. Her throat was dry. He had come to tell
her she must send the children to their grandparents.
That they were old and fussy and driven to exasperation
by more than three or four hours of the children's
company didn't matter. Peter had decreed their future
and Peter was their father. And, with that deadly
efficiency that he had brought to organising all their
childish games, as she remembered, he had not commit-
ted his orders to paper but had sent a messenger charged
with instructions to turn all their lives upside down.

'Go on,' she said in a chill little voice.

'I'd rather you came back and sat down. It's not
easy.'

'Is that why you've put it off for—how long? Three
weeks, is it? Couldn't you face me before?' she flashed.

He looked rueful. 'Well, I hardly got an enthusiastic
reception. And that was even before you knew who I
was.' He stood up. 'Look, we can work something out.
Don't get upset.'

He came towards her. Lucy whipped round, bracing
herself.

'I am not,' she said determinedly, 'upset. I gather
Peter has asked you to deliver the children to their
grandparents. I have nothing to say except that I shan't
do anything until I've written to Peter. Do I make myself
clear? And now perhaps you'll go.'

He ignored her, taking her hands and urging her on to
the window seat. 'Stop shaking,' he said kindly. 'Peter

didn't tell me to do anything of the kind, and if he had I wouldn't have agreed. Stop torturing yourself. What on earth gave you such an idea?'

'You—you wouldn't?' She drew the back of a shaking hand across her mouth in a childish gesture which returned in moments of stress. 'But—Peter said—I mean, I had a letter from him. . .'

'Then he must have explained.'

She shook her head. 'No. It—well, it was rather vague, I suppose. I took it to mean he wanted the children to go back to Elaine's parents. He was complaining about the village school. Oh, yes, and he said Boy needed a stable figure in his life.' She sniffed sorrowfully. 'What else was I to think?' she demanded, aggrieved.

'Did he indeed?' He sounded startled. Then he released her hands. 'I see your confusion. Peter doesn't seem to be any better at explaining himself than I am. He gave me a letter to deliver to you which I hope says it all better. But it would probably be best to give you a brief run-down first—then at least I can stop you jumping to unwelcome conclusions,' he added drily.

He went back to the fire and stood, with his hands behind his back, looking into the flames. 'I don't know quite how to put it. It sounds rather insulting. You see, Peter's worried about the children. They've done lots of tests on him—and they're doing more. He's not in bed all the time or anything drastic like that. It's simply that he can't shake off this infection and the doctors haven't identified it yet. Apparently he's been fretting badly at the lack of progress. That's why I was—er—asked to go and see him.'

She stared at him.

'He was—very excited. He said that something permanent had to be done about the children, that they couldn't go on living as temporary guests with you. He didn't think it was fair to you, among other things. So he suggested—that——' He took a deep breath, and said simply, 'He wants them to go away to school.'

'Away?' Lucy was uncomprehending. 'You mean boarding school? *Both* of them? But they're so little. They'd hate it. Oh, he can't do that!' She rose angrily to her feet. 'And you can't do that. I won't let you. I'll telegraph Peter. I'll see my lawyer tomorrow. You *can't*. . .'

'I can,' he said calmly. 'Or rather, I could if I judged it right. Peter has made me their guardian in his absence from England. I showed the deed to my solicitor as soon as I got back to England—that's really why I haven't spoken to you before. I wanted to know what our respective legal positions were. My solicitor says that he thinks you have a good case if you want to fight it. Courts are usually sympathetic to women parted from their ewelambs, apparently.'

Lucy flung her head up at that. 'Don't you dare to sneer at me!' she whispered.

'I'm not sneering. God knows, I don't blame you for feeling bitter.' He sounded very tired. 'I'm just trying to point out that you aren't helpless. You do have some redress if you feel that strongly. But—I'm told—the process is slow and costly. It would be better for everyone, not least the children, if we can come to some sort of arrangement.'

Lucy found humiliatingly that she wanted to cry. She turned her back on him, groping for a handkerchief. 'What sort?'

Robert Challenger laughed, heartlessly she thought. 'I hardly think there'd be any point in discussing it tonight. You're not in a mood to agree to anything. You'll be sticking pins in a wax image of me as soon as I've gone out of that door. Leave it till tomorrow. I'll come and see you.'

'I don't want to see you again,' she snapped childishly.

'I'm sure you don't,' he said with maddening sympathy. 'But that's hardly practical, is it? I'll leave you Peter's letter.'

He held it out to her, but she kept her back firmly turned away. Sighing, he put it on the arm of a chair.

'Coincidence!' she said bitterly. 'I don't believe in it. What about those milk bottles? I bet you broke them yourself just to have an excuse to get in here. And the house—how did you come to buy a house here?'

He shrugged. 'Dracula's Palace?'

'Don't call it that,' she snapped. 'It's beautiful.'

'It's old,' he allowed. 'Oh, come on, be sensible. We can't fight about a house.'

'It's a lovely old house. I suppose you can't appreciate it.'

'It has been,' he said pacifyingly. 'Now it's damp, it's got dry rot which the whole place reeks of, it's filthy and it's infested with rats.'

'So why buy it?'

He grinned. 'It appeals to my romantic soul.'

'You bought it so you could come and spy on me, didn't you? Is Peter paying for it?'

He strode forward and swung her round by the shoulders. 'Enough,' he said grimly, 'is enough. I make every allowance for your natural shock——' He saw the tears trickling down her cheeks and added in more moderate tones, 'I wanted a house. I've no ties in England. This seemed a nice enough place and Dracula's Palace took my fancy. Anyway, it's natural enough to want to be near the children, isn't it, if I'm responsible for them?'

'You are not,' she said between her teeth, 'responsible for them.'

'In law I am. And financially I am. Trust funds are being set up for them, and I shall be a trustee.'

For a speechless moment she looked up into his calm face. Behind the glasses he seemed to be laughing at her. She took a step back out of his imprisoning hands and, very deliberately, dealt him a ringing blow. The back of her hand smarted. She cradled it in the other one, appalled, waiting for retribution that she was sure would follow.

The glasses glittered down at her. He had seen it coming and dodged, but not quickly enough, and there was now a dull red mark along his cheek. For a brief moment she held her breath.

Then he said with great control, 'You're upset. I'll leave you. But if you ever try to do that again, I shall return it with interest.'

She backed away. 'I'm sure you would,' she said with disdain. 'However, the occasion won't arise. I shan't touch you again. I'm sorry I—forgot myself.'

'So am I,' he said ruefully. Then he smiled at her forgivingly. 'Never mind, I'm sure I deserved it. Let's say we're quits and start again. Can't we be friends?'

She snorted. 'Hardly.'

Unexpectedly he took her face between his hands. 'You know, you're a termagant,' he informed her. 'And Peter told me you were a quiet little thing who wouldn't give me any trouble. He underestimated you.'

'I hope so,' she returned viciously. 'I have every intention of giving you as much trouble as I can.'

'I can well believe it.' His mouth suddenly twitched in that unexpected, disrespectful laughter with which she was becoming familiar. 'Oh, well, in for a penny,' said Robert Challenger cheerfully, and kissed her.

Simple amazement held her still. She was still standing, dazed, when she heard the front door close gently behind him.

Lucy opened her eyes—which she could not recall having shut—swallowed and sat down shakily. The man was, of course, quite insufferable. He was impertinent, interfering and, to crown it all, he did not even seem to take her seriously. How dared he treat her as if she were some little mouse to sit quietly at home while he and Peter arranged her life to suit themselves? He had not even listened to her objections. Above all, how dared he walk out on that light, insulting kiss as if that was all that was needed to pacify her?

For a moment the greater issue was lost in the lesser one as she sat and fumed. Then common sense prevailed and she stretched out her hand for the letter. It was written on thin airmail paper and the envelope had the title and insignia of an American hospital inscribed on it. Lucy slit it open with great precision. It seemed to her that the very act of opening the letter was a sign of weakness. She felt she had acquiesced in Peter's remote plans. No doubt Peter, who did not think highly of the good sense of women in general and sisters in particular, would have instructed her to trust everything to his ambassador. In short she was to hand all their lives into the care of a flippant stranger. Miserable and mutinous, she unfolded the thin sheets and began to read.

It was much as she expected. Peter wrote with great affection but, as always, as if at least two-thirds of his mind were elsewhere. First of all he gave her a factual account of his symptoms which Lucy skipped without conscience. Then he commented unfavourably upon the spelling and handwriting of his offspring and attributed both to Lucy's own erratic habits in that direction. He added a terse criticism of the village school, which brought him to essentials. In two brief sentences, as Lucy noted in gathering wrath, he disposed of the children's future, consigning them together with their incompetent aunt to the care of Robert Challenger. He was her loving brother. That was all. Lucy searched in vain for any account of Robert Challenger. There was no description of him, no history, however lightly sketched. Above all there was no reason given for his election to the guardianship of the children. Who he was, or why he was judged suitable for that office, was ignored.

Lucy let the letter fall from her hands, torn between distress, annoyance, and a rueful half-desire to laugh. It was, of course, exactly the sort of letter Peter would write, indeed had always written. His infrequent epistles from school to their father had had just that ability to go straight to the heart of the matter. Comments upon the unvarying menu and the wildly various performances of the sports teams of which he was a member were invariably followed by crisp requests for such essentials as his piece of coral or his Mickey Mouse pencil-sharpener to be despatched with all speed.

She cast a disparaging look at his latest missive and cast it from her. In spite of her unwilling amusement she was disturbed. She began to move restlessly about the room, tidying magazines and plumping up cushions. It was all very well to laugh and in a way it was reassuring to know that Peter had not changed so much as might have been expected in the three years since she had last seen him. But these latest Olympian commands concerned more than his own well-ordered life.

She subsided into a chair, her head in her hands. What was she to do? She looked uncertainly at the telephone. She could hardly telephone Peter at this hour of night. Indeed, she had no idea what the time might be in San Francisco, now she came to think of it. And if she did telephone, always assuming she could discover the number of the hospital and Peter was available to talk to her and not asleep or on the operating table—what was she to say to him? He had always been more fluent than she was and would certainly have all his arguments ready to hand. Whereas she had nothing but a strong feeling of indignation at his cavalier treatment and a deep fear of the effect that his plans would have on the children, which was the most important thing of all, of course, and which she would find almost impossible to put into words. Particularly with a plausible and impatient Peter on the other end of a very expensive telephone line.

Lucy bit her lip. Where else could she go—for advice if nothing else? She had no doubt that her solicitor would corroborate what Robert Challenger had said. He was, she reflected angrily, by far too sure of himself to be mistaken on the subject. She began to nibble a fingernail. Mrs Browning would listen with enthusiastic sympathy, but there was nothing she could do. And as for Nicholas—Lucy sighed. Nicholas was a charming confidant when he had the time, but his advice was generally of an impractical nature. A great one himself for grand gestures without regard to the consequences or the people he offended by them, he had little patience with Lucy's more modest way of going to work. And at the moment, she thought wryly, he would not have the time even to listen.

She took her woes to bed with her and as a result hardly slept.

In the end she told nobody. For the rest of the week Colonel Browning kept her busy preparing the farm accounts. When she was not actually typing them out she was speeding about the farm collecting costings and production figures from the farm manager and his assistants. Mrs Browning, who continued to pursue her plans for a Jacobean entertainment with unabated fervour, was a little put out to find her accustomed amanuensis so very thoroughly occupied. She even took her husband to task for overworking his secretary.

Lucy for her part was glad of the work. She even took the accounts home with her and pored over them when the children were in bed. Financially the farm was in a disastrous state. Until he had come to look at his affairs in the light of the new loan he was trying to raise Colonel Browning had not realised how very grave matters were. Lucy pitied him extremely. She flung herself into the fray, frequently working past midnight.

But however much her work might absorb her during waking hours she could not control her thoughts when she was, supposedly, resting. She spent countless hours, cold and wakeful, revolving in her mind various imposs- ible alternatives. She could betake herself to the law, she might run away with the children. But the law was expensive and uncertain, and if she ran away somebody would be bound to find her. She was helpless and she knew it. She tried to be philosophical—perhaps the children *would* do better in boarding schools with others of their own age—but she knew too well how disturbed they were by the prolonged absence of their father and their mother's death to believe it. For both of them, Hazel Cottage and Lucy represented the only security they had ever found. It would be cruel to send them away.

And then she would fall into a light sleep full of nightmares of the children being persecuted and aban- doned and would wake up, her heart thumping furiously with the panic of her dreams.

She grew noticeably haggard. By Friday evening her eyes were dark-rimmed with sleeplessness and her face looked pinched. Adelaide Browning was concerned. Coming into the farm office at three o'clock, she found Lucy sitting at the typewriter staring blankly before her.

'*Lucy*. My dear!' she exclaimed, hurrying forward. 'Whatever is it?'

'What?' Lucy was shaken out of her reverie. 'Oh, hello, I'm sorry, I was miles away.'

'Outer Siberia, from the looks of it,' said Mrs Browning shrewdly. 'You're not letting Tom's miseries get you down, I hope?'

'No, of course not,' she murmured, beginning to tidy the typed sheets beside her.

'Because you mustn't. Even if we have to sell the farm, life goes on. Though Tom doesn't believe it, I know. But he would be just as happy in a cottage growing his own cabbages. Farms are too mechanised nowadays. All the fun's gone out of them. So you mustn't be downhearted about Tom.'

Lucy regarded her fondly. As she well knew, leaving the farm would be a major tragedy to Adelaide. 'I'm not,' she assured her.

Adelaide perched on the edge of her husband's desk. 'Then why the gloom? It's not like you. When I came in just now you had what my old grandmother would have called a face to fright the devil. Is it because you're overtired? Or just the October blues?'

'Both,' said Lucy uncommunicatively.

'What you need,' Adelaide informed her, 'is some fresh air. You don't get out enough.'

'It's hardly the weather for it,' pointed out Lucy, amused.

'Don't quibble. Air is air, even if it does come a little cold and damp at this time of year. Don't you ever go riding these days?'

Lucy sighed. While far from being an accomplished horsewoman, she had taken great delight in riding occasionally. Before the children came to live with her she would often hire a horse for the day from the village riding stables and take a picnic on to the hill. Valerie Dale who ran the school was a childhood friend and sometimes she and her husband or Nicholas Browning would join Lucy. It had stopped with the advent of the children because neither of them could ride, and Lucy had soon found that to leave them for a whole day, even in the care of easygoing Mrs Marshall at the farm, was to unsettle them for days.

'Have you stopped riding altogether?' Adelaide insisted.

'Oh, well, I didn't really have time. And anyway, the stable is so busy nowadays, I'd be lucky if Val could lend me Brown Robin for more than an hour. And I wouldn't want to trot sedately over the bridle paths. When I go riding I like to get away.'

'Humph,' said Mrs Browning, indicating dissatisfaction. 'Well, I don't care what you say. I think you ought to get out, for a couple of hours at least. I shall,' inspired, 'tell Nicholas to see to it.'

Lucy swallowed. It was in part a source of great comfort to her that Mrs Browning was not aware of her foolish affection for her nephew. On the other hand it did occasionally give rise to rather painful situations.

'No, thank you,' said Lucy firmly.

'Oh, but that's just what you need,' Adelaide assured her. 'You'll never have the resolution to go down to the stables and ask Val yourself. Every time it occurs to you there will be just something you have to do first. Or else you'll be so tired you'll put it off till tomorrow. But if somebody else is coming with you—it's entirely different.' She spread her hands. 'Don't you see? If Nicholas were waiting for you, you'd *have* to go.'

'Yes indeed,' said Lucy with wry self-mockery. 'And that might be very inconvenient. Besides, hasn't it occurred to you that he might have other things to do? He might not even want to come riding with me.'

'Nonsense,' said Adelaide briskly. 'It'll do him good. He's been looking distinctly peaky. *I* think it's that new chef they've got at the Royal Oak. Have you seen him?'

Lucy shook her head. 'No. I met the waitress, though. Nicholas told me they came together. She's lovely. Is she his wife?'

'Good heavens, no. She's not really a waitress at all. She's an actress, Nicholas tells me. The new chef's sister, I believe. She was saying that she had just finished a summer season in some provincial theatre and couldn't get another job. Apparently it's always hard at this time of year. So she went looking for her brother to keep her, of course, and Nicholas takes her in.' Adelaide sighed. 'That boy has a heart of gold.'

Lucy looked at her incredulously. It seemed to her that even his fond aunt must have noticed that Nicholas was enchanted by his new employee. Adelaide returned her look defiantly.

'He just hasn't the heart to turn people away,' she added.

Lucy choked. 'Er—he did need a waitress,' she murmured. 'And she's very pretty.'

Adelaide sniffed. 'Not to my way of thinking. She's too thin and she hasn't got any eyebrows.'

Irresistibly, Lucy began to chuckle. Adelaide surveyed her for an offended moment before she too laughed.

'I know I'm a cat,' she said without obvious contrition. 'But she looks quite appalling.'

Essentially fair-minded, Lucy had to disagree. 'I thought she looked rather pretty,' she remarked. 'More than pretty.'

Adelaide snorted. 'Nonsense! She looks like one of

those fairy tinsel dolls we put on top of the Christmas tree. They're just fancy wire if you take them to pieces. No substance to them.'

'Coo,' said Lucy. 'You really didn't like her, did you?'

Adelaide sighed. 'Oh, I'm fairly indifferent. Or I would be if Nicholas weren't such a *fool*.' She broke off and began to pleat her skirt absorbedly. 'We went there for dinner last night,' she continued, adding with a flash of mischief, 'That's why my poor Tom has been like a bear with a sore head all day. He doesn't get on with Provençal cooking.'

'Then why did poor Tom agree to go?'

'Because I told him we had to or Nicholas would be offended,' said Adelaide fluently.

'Oh!' Lucy was taken aback.

'The truth is, of course, that I wanted to see her. My spies told me that there was the most ravishing waitress at the Royal Oak, so of course I wanted to go and see. Nicholas is *besotted*.' She brooded. 'But then he so often is, poor boy. And always with the most desperately unsuitable women.'

Lucy managed to smile. 'Well, be honest. Who in your opinion *would* be suitable for Nicholas?'

Adelaide shrugged pettishly. 'Oh, I don't know. Somebody he hasn't found yet, obviously. Not one of these sharp little town creatures he's so fond of. Somebody who knows about village life and the land and would be happy here.'

'Perhaps the new waitress is just a simple milkmaid underneath,' suggested Lucy with false cheerfulness. 'Wait and see. She may surprise you.'

'Don't be obstructive,' snapped Adelaide on a little

spurt of temper. 'You know perfectly well what I mean. Men are such fools. He'd do much better with you.'

'I doubt it,' said Lucy with commendable equanimity. She looked at her watch. 'I don't want to hurry you, Adelaide, but I've got some things I must do before I go and meet the children. Did you want something special or did you just drop in for a chat?'

'Both,' said Mrs Browning promptly.

Lucy fed the paper into her typewriter and waited. 'Well?' she queried at length.

'It's a little difficult,' began Adelaide. 'You see, it's about this scheme of mine.'

'Oh, yes?' Lucy was noncommittal.

'I know I said I didn't want you to do any of the organising, and I meant it—at the time.'

'At the time,' said Lucy hollowly. 'Yes. Only now you do. What exactly do you want me to do?'

'Well, it's really that I want you to come and hold my hand while I do,' admitted Adelaide honestly.

Lucy stared at her.

'That beastly man at the Manor,' she explained. 'He's never there. And when I finally tracked him down on the phone he said I could go up tomorrow if I wanted, but he didn't sound very—welcoming.'

'He wouldn't,' said Lucy grimly.

'In fact he sounded positively hostile.' Adelaide looked at Lucy appealingly. 'Of course, I could go on my own. I mean, he's *asked* me—but I'd much rather have someone with me.'

'Me?' said Lucy in unfeigned horror. 'Oh, Adelaide, no!'

'But you've met him,' urged that lady, wheedling.

'You've talked to him.'

Lucy gave a short unamused laugh. 'Oh, I've talked to him all right,' she agreed. 'He is, without exception, the most detestable, arrogant, unfeeling man I've ever met!'

Adelaide blenched. 'Then you *can't* let me go and beard him on my own. It would be too unkind of you.'

'You're used to it,' said Lucy brutally. 'You have the knack of charming evil-tempered county councillors. Use the same technique on Mr Challenger.'

'I don't think I dare,' said Adelaide frankly. 'He looks so very——' She sought in vain for a word.

'Unpleasant?' supplied Lucy.

Adelaide considered it. 'No, not unpleasant. I wouldn't have said he looked exactly *nasty*. We saw him at the Royal Oak last night, you know. He eats there every evening, apparently, and he was quite civil. It's just that he's a bit awe-inspiring. I think urban is the word I want. You know, one of those people that picks up the telephone and gets things done. The sort of man,' said Adelaide wistfully, 'that one doesn't say no to. I bet nobody ever keeps *him* waiting in all day for gas men who don't turn up.'

This was an old grievance and Lucy laughed. 'I think that's a sort of Act of God, like earthquakes,' she said. 'I'm sure the Gas Board's no respecter of persons. Gas men don't turn up for everybody; all men are equal in their eyes.'

'Then he'd probably do the job himself,' averred Mrs Browning. 'He looks that sort of man. Capable.'

'And stupid? No one in their right mind fiddles around with gas.' Lucy was exasperated. 'Oh, this is a silly conversation. I don't see why you can't go and see Mr

Challenger about this idea of yours without making up all sorts of gruesome stories about him to frighten yourself out of it.'

'That's because you have no imagination,' retorted Adelaide. 'If you could only see him as I see him you'd know why. He has an aura. I am very sensitive to people's auras.'

'In that case, why not write him a letter and not have to see him—er—aura to aura, at all?' demanded Lucy sensibly.

'Because then he'd say no,' said Mrs Browning with simple truth. 'Oh, *please* come with me, Lucy. You needn't say anything. I'll do all the talking. But it would be such a relief to have someone with me. And you'd be ideal. You're so sensible. No matter how much you may dislike him, you're not in awe of him.'

She went to the door while Lucy watched her helplessly.

'I'll pick you up after lunch tomorrow. I really am very grateful. I know it sounds silly, but I really am quite frightened of him.'

The door closed gently behind her. Lucy sat and stared at it in dismay.

'And am I not?' she thought. 'God help me, am I not, too?'

CHAPTER FOUR

IF LUCY had slept little during the last few nights she did not close her eyes at all that night. At half-past three she gave up the unequal struggle and went downstairs. The last few embers were glowing in the fire and she added another log to the powdery hearth and blew the cinders into a rudimentary flicker.

She made herself some hot chocolate and sat over the fire, sipping this comforting brew and trying to make up her mind what she would say to Robert Challenger. He had promised to come and see her, she remembered, but he had not done so. Possibly her blatant hostility had persuaded him it would be useless. Perhaps he simply was not concerned with her at all. He could just drive up and carry the children off whenever he felt like it, thought Lucy, who always grew lachrymose in the small hours.

Yet something had to be said—even, she thought wryly, if only to concede defeat. It was inconceivable that she should invade his house in Adelaide Browning's train, listen meekly while that lady discoursed on Jacobean masques and heaven knew what else besides, and then simply leave without further reference to the children's welfare. She dwelled on the picture she conjured up for herself, and it filled her with embarrassed foreboding. She was nearly sure that it would inspire Robert Challenger with unholy amusement.

She gritted her teeth and tried to think of some way out of the tangle, but she was unsuccessful, and she eventually drifted into an uneasy sleep curled up on the hearthrug, one arm crooked on the seat of the armchair and her head bowed among its cushions.

It was in that position that the alarmed children discovered her the next morning.

'Lucy, Lucy!' gasped Boy, shaking her arm energetically. 'What's wrong?'

She stirred painfully, for her sleep had not been peaceful, and she awoke to a bitterly cold room and cramped limbs. But she was quick to sense their panic and to respond to it, even in her drowsy state.

'I couldn't remember whether I'd put the guard in front of the fire,' she lied, 'so I came down to see about it and fell asleep, that's all. What's the time?'

Angela was reassured. 'Late,' she said with satisfaction. 'We've been up ages.'

Boy, however, was still suspicious. 'Why didn't you put the guard up and go back to bed?' he demanded, swinging Lucy's hand roughly.

She blinked. 'Why——? Oh, I suppose I was just too tired. I just sat down and nodded off.'

'But why——?' he began, but she interrupted him, her impatience only half simulated.

'Oh, please, Boy, forget it. It doesn't matter why. All that matters is that as a result of my own stupidity I've slept badly and you'll have your breakfast late.'

She stood up painfully. Boy let go her hand, scowling. Both children, who would normally have run off to the farm by this hour or gone down the lane to meet the postman, stayed very close to her. The kitchen was a large one and Lucy did not normally find it inconvenient, but, flanked by two small but determined sentries, she discovered it was not nearly as large as she had formerly thought.

At last, in desperation after breaking her second egg of the morning, she suggested, 'Why don't you go and sit by the window and tell me when the postman is coming?'

This activity amused them endlessly on days which were too wet for them to go outside and meet him. They usually had a competition for the first to make it to the kitchen to announce to Lucy his imminent arrival and the winner was allowed to pour Johnny Postman's tea into his own special red mug. He used to laugh and say that Lucy had never had his Saturday morning tea ready poured and waiting on the table for him until the children came to live with her. The children were proud of the office and would not normally have abandoned it. Angela indeed seemed half ready to take up her station in the window, but Boy vetoed it.

'No, thank you, Lucy,' he said politely. 'It's cold in the sitting-room.'

Exasperated and a little worried, she did not try to persuade them. They ate their breakfast in near silence. Johnny Postman came, had his tea and commented upon their subdued faces, and left. Both of them refused to go out of the cottage, although it was a bright clear day. They sat side by side in front of the fire, lit nearly two hours later than usual, doing a desultory jigsaw puzzle and bickering because they were bored. Lucy was too glad to be left alone to do her housework to complain, but as soon as the telephone rang they were at her elbow, peering anxiously at the receiver as if they could see there the portrait of the caller.

It was Adelaide Browning, which seemed to relieve them, and they fell away, going back to the fire and their squabbles.

'About this afternoon,' said Adelaide.

'Yes?' said Lucy with foreboding.

'Could we possibly take your car? The Mini's radiator has blown up and I hate driving the Land Rover.'

'All right,' said Lucy, sighing. 'What time?'

'As soon after lunch as possible. Before I lose my nerve.'

Lucy shuddered. 'Don't be so silly,' she said with unwonted sharpness. 'It won't be for some time. I got up late and I've been behindhand all morning. The children won't want lunch until two at the earliest. Say about half-past three. I'll come and pick you up.'

'Oh, very well,' said Adelaide, plainly not pleased. 'But don't blame me if we have to stay for tea.'

'Well, it will hardly be made of hemlock, if we do,' observed Lucy, preparing to put the telephone down.

Faintly from the other end of the wire came Mrs Browning's parting shot. 'I wouldn't be too sure,' she said.

Slightly to Lucy's surprise the children were happy enough to be left after lunch. They knew she was going out with Mrs Browning and this was familiar enough to be unalarming. Boy went off to play with Billy Marshall and Lucy dropped Angela at the riding school on her way to the Brownings'. Both of them seemed to have recovered from the morning's upset, but they had been more disturbed by finding her downstairs than she would have expected, and she frowned. She cast a look in her driving mirror, but Angela was not standing waving at the gates but had hopped cheerfully inside with her friends without so much as a glance behind her. Lucy bit her lip. She felt she ought to be relieved at such resilience, but instead the children's very volatility was beginning to worry her.

She turned in at the gates of the home farm and stopped her old car in the drive. Taking the shortest route, she went through the office into the stableyard and across to the kitchen door. The house had been built as a dower house to serve the eighteenth-century squire's importunate mother-in-law whose shrill ghost was still supposed to haunt her sewing-room. Since that date it had come down in the world and was now a somewhat rambling and untidy farmhouse. Lucy, who had known it since her childhood, loved it. Nevertheless she could see that it was becoming shabbier with every year that passed as Colonel Browning struggled to keep the estate together. The stables were empty now apart from the indigenous chickens which kept the Brownings and the Wilds supplied with eggs.

For a moment she stood looking round the empty yard. In the dark October afternoon it was bleak. She shivered.

'Lucy!'

She looked up at the imperative voice. Adelaide Browning was leaning out of an upstairs window.

'Don't stand there mooning. You'll freeze. Trot on, there's a good child.'

'Sorry,' she said, laughter suddenly lighting her eyes. 'Are you ready?'

'Yes, yes,' said Adelaide speciously. 'Just come up for

a moment, will you. I want your advice.'

'What about?' asked Lucy, standing her ground.

'Well, I'm not quite sure about this scarf,' began Adelaide, and broke off, hurt, as Lucy shook her head reprovingly.

'Come along, Adelaide. Courage!'

'I don't know what you mean,' began Mrs Browning huffily, but Lucy interrupted her.

'Yes, you do. You're trying to put it off. I am *not* going to be lured indoors for a dressing-up session. You wanted to talk to the ogre. You've got an appointment. You've got a chauffeur. You can't chicken out now.'

'Oh, very well,' said Mrs Browning, withdrawing her head from the window. 'You're a hard girl, Lucy Wild.'

In two minutes she appeared in the kitchen doorway, looking very elegant in a tailored suit with a bright scarf knotted audaciously at her throat. Lucy, who was wearing serviceable tweed trousers and a favourite soft lichen-green sweater, suddenly felt dowdy.

'Oh, well, let's go and get it over with,' said Adelaide. 'But I warn you, I'm terrified.'

Nobody, thought Lucy, would have guessed it. Still less would they have suspected it seeing Mrs Browning greet her host serenely when she stepped out of Lucy's battered car not half an hour later.

She apologised prettily for bringing along an uninvited companion, explaining her own car was out of commission and Lucy had been kind enough to offer her own, making it sound, thought Lucy resentfully, as if it had been her idea rather than Adelaide's. After one startled glance at her, Robert Challenger had seemed indifferent enough.

'But of course, you've already met Lucy,' said Adelaide, fishing delicately.

'Yes, of course. How do you do, Miss Wild? Won't you both come in? I'm afraid the house is still rather a junkyard, but there's a fire in the library. And that's really all that's needed to make a house habitable in this sort of weather, isn't it?'

They followed him, Adelaide chatting politely, Lucy silent. He held the library door open for them, giving Lucy a quick look as she passed him, half-irritated, half-amused. She affected not to notice.

As he had said the room was still only half furnished, with two large wooden chests standing against the window. He drew a chair, obviously swept clear of books and packages especially for Mrs Browning's arrival, to the fire.

'Please sit down,' he said, looking vaguely round for another chair for Lucy.

She saw a little footstool beside the grate and sat on that. Seeing her choice, Robert Challenger looked relieved and leaned against the fine old marble mantelpiece, careless of the dust and paper shavings on it. His elbow, thought Lucy dispassionately, would be coated in dirt. She pitied whoever had to wash his sweaters.

'Well, Mrs Browning, now that you've found me, what can I do for you?'

Adelaide was rather put out by his direct approach, Lucy observed. She would have preferred to pretend hers was merely a neighbourly visit before she plunged into the purpose of it.

'It's a little difficult to explain,' she began after a brief moment to collect herself. 'I don't suppose it will mean much to you unless you know anything of our local history.'

'Not a thing,' he said cheerfully.

'Oh. Well.' Adelaide looked desperately at Lucy for help.

It was not in her nature to refuse it. 'There's a Roman Way along the hill,' she explained quietly. 'At least there was. Now it runs through two fields which belong to a private company which refuses to admit a public right of way through them. We've fought it in the courts and gone as far as we could, but it would be very expensive to take it any higher. The obvious thing is to buy the fields in question.'

He nodded. 'I can see that. But what has that to do with me? I don't own any land on the hill, as far as I'm aware.'

Adelaide spoke again. 'Funds,' she pronounced.

'Ah, I see.' He was blantantly amused now. 'Of course, I shall be delighted to help.' He looked round the room again rather helplessly. 'When I can locate my cheque-book. It's here somewhere, I'm sure. I must ask——'

'Good heavens, we don't want *money*,' exclaimed Adelaide, quite shocked.

He stopped his search. '*Don't* want money?' He looked at Lucy. 'Then what the devil do you want?'

Adelaide looked flustered. 'Your house,' she said baldly.

'*My house*?'

Feeling rather superior—and very mean because of it—Lucy interposed quietly, 'Mrs Browning thought that she might be able to raise money for the Roman Way appeal by giving a public entertainment here—as it's the oldest house in the village.'

'Here?' He looked round eloquently. 'Old it most certainly is, it's tumbling about our ears. But it's hardly Roman.' He looked at Adelaide, fascinated. 'What sort of entertainment?'

'Oh, something Jacobean, we thought,' she replied airily, basely suggesting Lucy's implicit support. 'A spot of singing—the Vicar conducts a rather good madrigal group. Perhaps the children might do a nativity play if it were at Christmas. The amateur dramatic society might care to do a scene or two from something suitable. . .'

Lucy, perceiving the gathering horror in his face, was hard put to it not to laugh. Adelaide did not observe it, and wove her fantasies on while he stood as if transfixed by the mantelpiece, unable to take his eyes off her.

'. . .and Lucy plays the lute,' she finished triumphantly.

Robert Challenger closed his eyes fleetingly, and the smallest perceptible shudder went through him. He opened them and glanced reproachfully at Lucy who, brimful of mischief, looked innocently back.

'Come now, Mr Challenger,' Adelaide almost clasped her hands in supplication, 'what do you think?'

There was a slight pause while he seemed to be choosing his words.

'I think,' he said at length, carefully, 'it's a very— intriguing—idea. But as you can see——' he gestured largely '—there's hardly room for me here at the moment, let alone the school, the madrigal choir, the amateur dramatic society and the—er—public.'

Adelaide waved that aside. 'We'll all come and help

you get the place ready,' she assured him. 'Of course. Won't we, Lucy?'

He began to look harassed. 'You're very kind, but I already have as much—indeed more—help than I can use. It's not just a matter of cleaning up and hanging curtains, you see. There's a good deal of structural alterations to be done.'

'Before Christmas?' demanded Adelaide keenly.

'Well, no, I suppose not.'

'Then there's no reason why we shouldn't use the house before Christmas, provided we put it in order, is there? I mean, we wouldn't be damaging your new decorations or anything.'

'I suppose not,' he said again.

The door opened and he turned to it eagerly, like a man reprieved.

'Ah, here comes the help I was talking about,' he said. 'I think she's been brewing tea. I do hope,' to Adelaide, 'that you drink tea. It's the only non-alcoholic beverage in the house.'

The door opened fully and a girl appeared at it, carrying a large and loaded tray. Robert Challenger went across to take it from her.

'There's no need for you to wait on me,' he protested. 'You do enough of that in your professional capacity.'

It was Simone Russell. Her pretty hair tied back at the nape of a slender neck with a bow and her cheek faintly dusty, she looked as if she had been helping very comprehensively with his housework.

'Thank you,' she said as he took the tray. 'Good afternoon, Mrs Browning. Hello, Lucy. I hope you also like ginger nuts. He's got absolutely nothing in his pantry except ginger nuts and potato crisps.'

She laughed at him with so much open affection that Adelaide, exchanging startled looks with Lucy, was quite confounded.

'Does Nicholas know you're here?' she enquired impulsively.

Simone looked surprised. 'I don't know. Does it matter? I don't start work until seven, you know.'

'Oh, no. No, of course not,' murmured Adelaide. 'Forgive me.'

Challenger handed her tea. 'Simone's been over here a good deal,' he said with emphasis. 'She's really been very kind. I haven't been here all that much and she very kindly keeps a key and lets workmen into the place whenever I'm away.'

'You are fortunate,' said Adelaide, in measured tones, 'that she has such a very convenient job.'

He surveyed her with a good deal of comprehension. 'Aren't I?' he agreed gently.

Simone poured tea for Lucy and handed it to her. 'Oh, he's quite impossible,' she said with another laughing, intimate glance at their host. 'I never know when he's coming or going. He just disappears. This week, for instance, he suddenly took off. Then last night he appeared in the hotel for dinner without any warning. It's just as well he isn't married. No wife would stand for it.'

'No?' said Adelaide cattily, but Simone was impervious to insult. She looked like a little silken lapdog perched gracefully on the edge of a brimming piano stool. Her hair was quite as soft and shining as Lucy remembered it and her eyes were, if possible, larger. She

had a low voice and a hurried, breathless way of speaking
that made her sound like a solemn child. Her hands
fluttered all the time she was talking, to the imminent
danger of the teacup and the papers on which she had set
it. She was a fascinating little person. Nicholas at least,
Lucy was gloomily sure, would not fail to be fascinated.
Even in jeans and a dust-stained black shirt she had grace
and a certain style.

Lucy averted her eyes in case she was caught staring—
not that Simone would have noticed her regard or been in
the least disturbed by it if she had. Simone, very
obviously, had no eyes for anyone but her host. In his
turn he treated her rather as if she were a child, petted
and pretty, whom it amused him to indulge. He was very
unlike poor Nicholas, who looked quite foolish with love
whenever Simone appeared. And his technique, thought
Lucy viciously, seemed to have rather more success.
Seeing Simone purring and preening herself beside him,
Lucy was almost tempted to do something about it.

Adelaide meanwhile was trying to bring Robert
Challenger back to the point. He had so nearly suc-
cumbed, she was sure, before Simone entered. She took
him over the ground again very carefully.

Simone watched his face and seemed to only notice one
word in ten of what was being said, but she did prick up
her ears when she heard the word 'play'.

'Oh, are you going to do a play here?' she demanded
artlessly. 'In the great hall?'

'Great hall!' scoffed its proud owner. 'Draughty great
barn of a room. You could never heat it. The central
heating won't be installed in the main house until the
spring,' he explained to Adelaide triumphantly.

'Then we can use logs,' she replied with great serenity. 'That's what the Jacobeans must have used, after all. We've plenty of logs at the farm. You needn't worry on that score.'

'I won't,' he agreed. 'Mrs Browning, are you serious? You've seen the sort of state the place is in. Even the kitchen isn't fitted properly yet. How can you possibly hold any sort of function here? It would be a farce!'

She looked at him and was struck by a brilliant idea. 'Of course,' she mused. 'I should have seen it before.'

'Seen what?' said Lucy uneasily from her chimney corner. She had seen that look before.

'A farce. When Mr Challenger said that it would be a farce I saw at once what we ought to do. We must have a dance, a proper dance—you can see to all that, Lucy—but a *fancy dress* dance. We'll make people come dressed as characters out of comedies. Oh, it will be charming!'

Simone nodded enthusiastically. Robert Challenger looked like one who has been struck down when he least expected it. Thinking of what Colonel Browning would say to this latest flight of fancy, Lucy shuddered. But Adelaide had found a fellow enthusiast and was not to be stopped.

'We can have the entertainment quite early in the evening—after all, the mothers will want to get the children to bed after the nativity play. How late are your two allowed up, Lucy?'

'Eight o'clock,' said their aunt mendaciously.

'Oh, well, they'll just have to stay up a bit later for once. It'll be a treat for them,' said Adelaide dismissingly. 'But say they have to be in bed by ten. They could do their play at nine and then go home.'

'What time does the madrigal choir have to be in bed?' demanded Robert Challenger wickedly.

'Oh, they don't. They're grown up. They can,' said Mrs Browning, paying him out nicely in all innocence, 'go on to the small hours.'

'It's to be hoped they won't, though.'

'They're quite good,' Lucy assured him solemnly. He drew a long, patient breath. 'And it wouldn't matter if they weren't, because they're all related to half the county and all their friends and relations will come to hear them and pay good money into the Roman Way fund to do so,' she finished.

'You,' he said softly, looking down at her from his stance by the mantelpiece, 'are a very cynical young lady.'

'No, I'm not. Just practical. You want it to be a success, don't you?'

'Don't try my patience too far,' he warned. 'It's all very well for you to sit there looking demure. You know perfectly well I shan't be able to get out of it now. What a terrible woman!'

'Simone doesn't seem to agree with you,' she remarked.

Mrs Browning and Miss Russell were already engaged in a spirited exchange of views on a suitable scene to be performed. Mrs Browning had hitherto been the leading light of the amateur dramatic society, but it looked as if she would be so no longer. Lucy bit back a smile as they turned to Robert Challenger to adjudicate.

'*Twelfth Night*, or something more frivolous and eighteenth-century?' demanded Adelaide. 'What do you think, Mr Challenger?'

For the first time he seemed really at a loss. 'I—really I—I wouldn't have an idea, Mrs Browning. What do you think?' swinging round on Lucy sitting mumchance on her stool.

'Oh, eighteenth-century,' she assured them, with only the faintest tremor in her voice. 'Think what a beautiful age it was for dress. Nicholas would look lovely in a brocade waistcoat.' She paused and raised innocent eyes to Robert Challenger, as he towered over her. 'Perhaps you'll even be able to persuade our host to take part.'

There was a pause before Adelaide and Simone began to exclaim over the excellence of the idea. Lucy's victim meanwhile remained inscrutable.

Then he said, 'I can see I shall have to, as everyone else is going to. Nicholas, Simone, the Vicar—even your nephew and niece. And yourself, of course. I shall look forward to hearing you on the triangle.'

'Lute,' corrected Adelaide.

For one incredulous moment he stared at her and then his shoulders began to shake. 'Lute,' he said. 'Of course. How—how silly of me.'

Lucy, blushing furiously, glared at him.

'Only she never does play it for anybody,' complained Mrs Browning.

'Well, she'll have to this time, won't she?'

Lucy stared at him. It was a joke, a dare, a piece of mischief, and yet he made it sound faintly threatening. Mr Challenger, it seemed, did not care to be teased. She wondered briefly that Simone dared to treat him with such confident casualness. Then, before other disasters could strike, she left in Adelaide's wake, saying nothing more beyond a murmured goodbye—scuttling out, she

thought disgustedly, like a beetle caught away from its
stone. But she did not think she could outface him, and
given that, she did not dare to stay.

All that afternoon Lucy chided herself for her cowardice.
After all, they would have a good deal to say to one
another if he was, however unjustly, to be the children's
guardian. He had a right to expect her to discuss the
subject with him. After so unsatisfactory an interview, he
must surely seek her out. She did not look forward to it.

So when there was a knock at the door that evening,
her heart jumped into her mouth. She told the children
sharply to go and get ready for bed before she went to
open the door. Puzzled and suspicious, they trailed after
her, not quite disobedient but obeying her with the
absolute minimum of zeal that just stopped short of
defiance. Boy in particular trailed disconsolately upstairs
with many an uneasy glance over his shoulder.

It was something of an anti-climax to find the doorstep
full of Rusty with Nicholas Browning hovering apologet-
ically in the shadows behind him.

Instantly the dog bounded in, to be met by Angela, all
vestiges of obedience thrown to the winds, who leaped
down the stairs to meet him. Lucy's greeting was more
restrained. She patted Rusty's broad head and stood
aside for Nicholas to come in.

'You're out at an unseasonable hour,' she observed,
taking his coat from him. 'No customers tonight?'

'None that the others can't very well deal with on their
own.' He ran a hand through his tousled hair. 'I suddenly
felt I had to get out. The atmosphere was oppressive in
the restaurant. The customers had got round to coffee

and the place stank of cigars and cold food, and I just couldn't take any more. So I brought Rusty out for his walk early.'

Lucy raised her eyebrows but returned no comment. She led the way into the sitting-room which, as always after an evening with the children, was in total disorder. Nicholas, a little bewildered, picked his way across a floor strewn with cushions and diminutive vehicles to the fire. He sat down, his hands hanging loosely between his knees, staring absently before him. He looked tired and, Lucy thought, rather unhappy.

She went into the hall and quelled the children's romping. Ignoring their reproachful faces, she said firmly, 'Go upstairs and wash. You may come down and say goodnight in your dressing-gowns. But only,' with great emphasis, 'if you go up *now*.'

They went. Rusty padded after her and settled down at his master's feet, totally obscuring the fire. She hauled on his hindquarters—which, being an amiable beast, he did not appear to resent—until he was at right angles to his former position and seated herself opposite Nicholas. Rusty, quite happy as long as his nose remained in contact with Nicholas's shoes, gave a gusty sigh and closed his eyes. Lucy smiled.

'If only he were a fifth his present size that creature would be quite perfect,' she said.

Nicholas started. 'What? Oh, Rusty. Yes, he's a good soul.'

And he went off into his sorrowful reverie again.

Lucy sat quietly with her hands in her lap waiting for him to speak. She was not embarrassed by his silence, for she had known him too long. It was, besides, a rare pleasure to see him seated at her fireside, for he seldom left the Royal Oak in the evenings. For a moment, half ashamed, she played with the fantasy that they might be man and wife, the children upstairs their own, the whole of Sunday stretching peacefully before them. For a moment the picture was so strong—and so attractive— that she almost reached out to take his hand. Then he looked up and she drew back, blushing.

'What am I going to do, Lucy?' he said wretchedly. 'I'm in the most frightful mess, and it's all my own fault.'

Lucy clasped her hands strongly together and wished that he did not appeal to her quite so much.

'Most of the really bad messes usually are one's own fault,' she said dispassionately. 'What have you done—or not done—this time?'

For a moment she thought he wasn't going to answer her, and then he sprang up and went to the window. Rusty, dispossessed, growled, then sank his head on to his forepaws and slept again.

'I'm in love, Lucy,' Nicholas burst out. 'This time it's for real. And she——'

'She——?' prompted Lucy painfully.

'Oh, she's quite kind to me. She lets me tease her and take her out occasionally. But she doesn't really know it's me. It could be anyone—most of the time it is. She's so attractive, everyone wants her.' He laughed bitterly. 'Every time the telephone goes now it's one of her men. And she treats us all the same.' He smote his fist against the palm of his hand. 'I won't have it. It's not good enough. She must take me seriously. But what can I do? It's better to be one among many than not to have her at all.'